WHIPPED

Phoenix Williams

ISBN: 148101028X
ISBN-13: 978-1481010283

<u>DEDICATION</u>

This book is dedicated to those who are not afraid to embrace and indulge their innermost desires. It is also dedicated to those who do not deny themselves pleasure regardless of what society thinks.

PHOENIX WILLIAMS

TABLE OF CONTENTS

HOPELESSLY
ADDICTED

My name is Kimber and I am an addict. I'm addicted to my husband's dick. The sight of Dexter's dick in front of me makes my mouth water, pussy sing and heart flutter. I love the feel of it against my full lips, gliding across my tongue and tickling my tonsils. His salty sweetness dripping down my throat is the catalyst to my most powerful orgasms.

I could spend hours with his dick in between my lips and never complain. I don't need him to fuck me, just satisfy my oral habit and I'll be gloriously happy. My husband knows that he has me dick whipped. I need the taste of him on my tongue to get through the day.

To me, it isn't about the act itself but what it represents. It is a very intimate act, one of true power and raw possession. I am his and he is mine. Every inch of my body has been tasted and claimed by him. He is in my bloodstream, the sway of my

1

hips, the light in my eyes, the rise and fall of my breast and the flutter of my pussy.

For this, I want to show him he is appreciated. He knows that no matter how harsh the outside world is; there is a place where he will be worshipped like the king he is. That place is the home we have lovingly created together.

I am not the only addict in our marriage. Dexter is addicted to the sugar walls between my thighs almost as much as I am to the chocolate stick between his. Two oral addicts together is a recipe for cum showers and mishaps.

There have been a few instances where I wish one of us had been strong enough not to delve our heads in between each other's thighs. The top two occurrences that come to mind are when I almost got my husband fired from his job and when we almost gave my mom a heart attack.

I was off from work when the urge to taste Dexter hit me so strong that I had to leave the line at the DMV and drive straight to his office. Dexter worked as an executive at a manufacturing company in the suburbs of Chicago. He had a private office so I wasn't worried about being caught.

Bypassing the security guard at the front desk, I almost ran to the elevator in my gold and black six inch Fendi heels. When I arrived to his floor his secretary informed me that Dexter was scheduled to have a meeting in thirty minutes. I wasn't concerned. My head game was tight and I knew how to make my husband cum in less than ten minutes.

Walking into his office, his scent hit me first and caused my nipples to tighten against my chocolate silk blouse. From the first day I met him, it was his scent that always got to me. It was an intoxicating mixture of cologne and masculinity. Dexter flashed that pretty white smile at me and motioned for me to sit across from his desk as he finished up his phone call.

Sitting in the chair, I noticed how his eyes roamed to my long legs exposed by my short black skirt. I blushed. No matter how many years we were together, it always amazed me how he could still want me as if we had just met.

I allowed my gaze to admire the man I pledged my love to four years ago. Dexter was so handsome he could have been a Hollywood star if he wanted. Standing at 6'3" with deep chocolate skin, hazel eyes and a body that was muscular without being bulky; he demanded attention wherever he went. He kept his hair closely cropped and his face was baby smooth. He said he didn't like stubble irritating my sensitive skin. It was that sort of consideration, kindness, and awareness that made me want to do for him.

The soft click of the phone being placed in the cradle brought my attention back to why I was there.

"Hey baby, I didn't expect to see you until later tonight."

Licking my lips, I stared into his hypnotizing eyes before whispering, "I couldn't wait."

The darkening of his eyes let me know that he caught my meaning. "Kimber, baby, I have a meeting in less than twenty minutes."

"I don't care," I said standing.

With a sigh he leaned back in his chair. He knew that once my mind was made up there was nothing he could do about it. Rounding the desk, I crawled underneath. It was a tight fit since I was 5'9" and thick as hell.

Pushing my shoulder length hair out of my face, I got to work on his belt. A soft groan escaped him as I pushed down his soft linen slacks and silk boxers to his ankles. I moaned when I saw my prize, my drug. Looking him in his eyes, I lowered my mouth on to him.

We both moaned as inch after magnificent inch slipped past my lips into my hot, wet mouth. Relaxing my throat, I pushed all ten inches into my mouth while my tongue grazed his balls. I continued to look in his eyes as my head bobbed up and down in his lap.

He swept my bangs back and stared into my face. Pleasure rippled through me when his hips began to surge upward. Moisture dripped from my leaky pussy down my thick thighs to the carpeted floor. The cold air from the air conditioner breezing across my caramel ass caused another groan to escape my throat.

Taking my mouth off of him, I buried my face into the thatch of hair below his dick and inhaled. The fragrance of my man's excitement made me high. Sucking one then both balls in my mouth, I rotated them on my tongue as I gathered moisture from my pussy and rubbed it on his dick. Up and down I worked my wrist. In and out I worked my jaws. Back and forth Dexter worked his hips.

Abruptly, I released his balls and slammed my mouth back down his chocolate stick. Holding him in the back of my throat, I hummed while I firmly massaged his balls, only stopping when he closed his eyes. I needed to look in my husband's eyes while I pleasured him. The look of surrender on his face filled me with a sense of extreme power. To know that I could bring this strong and dominant man to his knees always stole my breath.

The taste of my pussy mixed with Dexter's own unique flavor, the aroma of our love mingling in the air, the feel of him inside my oral cavity and the look of tremendous pleasure in his eyes was too much for me. I squirted, soaking my panties, skirt and the floor beneath me.

Knowing that I had climaxed, he finally succumbed to my ministrations and gave me what I desperately craved. I tightened my hold on him making sure every ounce of the precious concoction landed on my tongue. I swallowed and slowed down my intense suction.

I watched in triumph as his head rolled back. I kept him lodged inside me and I gently scraped my nails across his thighs and balls. Giving the head one last kiss, I gently placed it back in the boxers, straightened his pants and redid his belt. I stood and straightened my skirt, before reapplying gloss to my swollen lips.

I leaned over to give my semi-comatose husband a kiss goodbye when the door suddenly opened. Dexter sat up in his chair as his colleagues walked in one by one, apparently ready to start their meeting. Dexter and I both watched as the five men and three women narrowed their eyes and flared their nostrils, the sweet smell of my pussy assaulting them. Admiration for Dexter and lust for me filled the eyes of the men; while disgust and jealousy filled the women's. Greeting everyone, I grabbed my purse before kissing Dex goodbye.

That night over a dinner of baked sole and citrus coleslaw, Dexter let me know how my visit affected the rest of his day.

"You almost got my ass fired today, Kimber," he said with laughter in his voice.

Swirling my wine in my glass, I looked at him through my lashes. "Really? How so?"

"Like you don't know! The men were cool with it. In fact, Hadley told me how he wished his wife would come visit him sometime." Sipping his wine he continued, "But the women, especially Margaret, were very upset. I was told that sex on the premises would not be permitted."

"You should have told them we didn't have sex, since we didn't."

"Oh, really? What should have I said? 'My wife didn't give me any pussy but she did suck me so good I wanted to crawl in the fetal position and suck my thumb.' Yeah, that would have been a whole lot better."

Rolling my eyes, I smiled. "I'm sorry baby," I said even though I wasn't. "I won't do it again."

"Not as sorry as I am. You'll never know how fucking sexy you looked under my desk, skirt around your waist, head in my lap and your ass in the air. Damn!! Every time I looked at my desk I thought of you."

Blowing him a kiss, I finished my meal. I knew at that moment, that what happened in his office would go in our top ten of memorable sexperiences.

My mother and I are very close. I spend almost every Saturday morning with her, while Dex hangs out with the guys golfing or trying to resurrect their basketball dreams.

This particular Saturday morning my mother needed my help baking three hundred cupcakes for the local elementary school's Valentine's Day festival. We had baked and frosted over two hundred when she had to leave for her hair appointment. I volunteered to finish up the rest and watched her leave. I texted Dex to let him know that I wouldn't be able to make our lunch date and he assured me that it was okay.

An hour later, I was in the middle of adding candy hearts to the latest batch of cupcakes when I heard the key slide through the lock on the front door. Glancing up, I saw my husband walk inside and my breath stalled in my chest. A blush stole my cheeks and butterflies took occupancy in my stomach. After all of these years he was still able to elicit this reaction from me.

Coming up from behind me, he wrapped his arms around me and brushed a kiss to the nape of my neck.

"Hey baby."

Hey honey, I thought you were still going to be with your boys, since I'm stuck here."
"Naw, they weren't feeling too well."

Leaning into his embrace, I looked in his eyes. "Did y'all get embarrassed on the courts again?" He suddenly couldn't meet my gaze. "You did, didn't you? See, I told all of you to stop with this nonsense. This is exactly what you get."

"Whatever girl, you know I still got game."

"I know you need to sit your thirty-four year old ass down somewhere and hang up the jersey. Hang up the jersey, baby!" I said with a laugh.

"Keep talking shit Kimber and I won't help you with all these cupcakes."

That quickly shut me up. With his help it would only take me half as long to finish the other batches of cupcakes. We worked in a comfortable silence, he frosting and me baking. Two hours passed before we had all the cupcakes baked, frosted, decorated and stored. We cleaned up the kitchen until the only things left out were the bowls of red, pink, and white frosting.

"Baby, thank you for the help because I would have still been here working," I said before kissing him.

I pulled back and turned towards the sink. I could feel his eyes on me and knew I was in trouble. His heat and scent reached me before he did. Placing both hands on my arms, he turned me towards him. The look in his eyes said it all. There was no need for words. A slight nod of my head was the only permission he needed. Dex slid his hands down my arms and settled them at the waistband of my shorts. Gathering my shorts and panties, he slowly stripped them from my body as he knelt before me.

Looking at my shaved pussy, he smiled. Standing, he tossed my shorts and panties aside before lifting my t-shirt above my head and unhooking my bra. Both items landed in the direction of the shorts and panties. Taking a step back, Dex leaned against the granite island and stared at me.

"Beautiful," he whispered ardently. "Absolutely beautiful."

Taking his shirt off, he made sure it joined the pile of clothing then returned his attention back to me. Lifting me up in his strong arms, he placed me on the island and spread me wide. I laid back, closed my eyes and waited for my man to take what he wanted, what he needed.

My eyes flew back open when I felt something cool touch my skin. Looking down, I saw that Dex was using the frosting to paint me, red on my nipples, white on my stomach and pink on my inner thighs.

Chuckling, he looked up at me. "Baby, this frosting is the same color as your pretty ass pussy."

Before I could respond he attacked my nipples. Licks, sucks and bites made my twin buds as hard as Hershey kisses. Excitement swirled in my belly and I writhed wildly against the cool granite. Dex's hot tongue devoured the red sugary substance before trailing towards my stomach causing it to contract violently in anticipation. Moans escaped my parted lips when his tongue dipped into my navel. Groans tore from his throat as he kissed and licked the place our future children would one day occupy.

Bringing a stool to the island, he sat down and pulled me to the edge of the counter. His strong hands massaged my thighs, coaxing me to relax and spread them wider. Juices trickled down my thighs, blending with the frosting creating sticky, saccharine syrup that was sure to send him into diabetic shock.

The moment Dex's tongue touched my inner thighs; my hips bolted upward on their own accord. A warning growl forced me to be still and enjoy the pleasure he was giving me. Placing myself on my elbows, I watched as he kissed and nibbled movement of my body as he held my hips in his strong hands. His tongue delved deeper and deeper into me, before moving up to flick my clit.

Fire and ice pumped through my veins, my vision blurred and legs began to shake as he got his fix. Dex drank deeply from the river he had created, slurping and swallowing the pussy sauce only he knew the recipe to.

Orgasm was on the horizon. I could feel it from the tips of my toes to my hair follicles.

Suddenly, he released me and removed that beautiful mouth from me. Cries of mourning left my lips as I reached for him.

Dex picked me up and set me on the floor forcing me to find my balance with shaky legs. Reaching between us, he placed two fingers inside me and pressed against my g-spot. Had it not been for his arm around me I would have fell to the floor. Kissing him deeply, I rode is fingers to get the orgasm I so desperately needed. Again he denied me.

Lying down on the counter, he looked at me. "Sit on my face baby," he whispered roughly.

Before he could finish the last word, I was kneeling over his stiff tongue ready to impale myself on it. Strong arms clasped soft thighs. Wet pussy met eager tongue. Screams were wrenched from souls and bodies convulsed with intense gratification. Dex's eyes rolled in the back of his head. This was what he needed. He needed to taste my desire for him, to know that he could still make me ache for him.

We found a rhythm that was as old as time yet uniquely us. My hips lightly bouncing up and down and his tongue furiously circling. Sweat dripped from my chest onto his forehead mingling with his. Dessert and arousal wafted into my nostrils, filling my head to the bursting point.

Dex shifted his mouth to my clit and kissed. Not just any kiss but a loud, wet, smacking kiss that caused my clit to jump. He kept kissing it even as my thighs held his head in a vice grip and my pussy bathed him. When the last spasms left my body I could only lean back and palm my nipples while he licked the excess moisture from me.

"OHMIGOD!!!!"

"Mama!" I screamed as I quickly jumped of Dexter.

"Girl, put some damn clothes on!" she exclaimed, her back turned.

Quickly Dex and I tried to make ourselves look presentable. Turning back towards us, my mother just looked at us with a look of shock and anger. Making her way to the counter top, she grabbed a napkin and handed to Dex. "Clean yourself up!" she hissed.

There we stood in a sex scented room before my very religious mother with rumpled clothes, mussed hair and with pussy juice dripping down Dex's chin. Of course he couldn't resist one last lick before wiping the remnants away.

"You two should be ashamed of yourselves. You're not a couple of teenagers who just discovered sex. You are very grown adults."

"Mama, we are so sorry," I said even though I wasn't. I was sorry we got caught.

"Not as sorry as you're going to be. I want…No, I need brand new counter tops. I can't cook or eat on these after they have been tainted with your sexcapade," she huffed before stomping upstairs.

Looking at Dex, a smile played around my lips. "How much you want to bet the entire neighborhood will know about this before the end of the day?"

"Baby, they'll know within the hour."

Grabbing the cleaner from beneath the cabinets, I sighed. "Dex, we should be ashamed of ourselves."

17

"Yeah, but we're not," he said while wiping down the counter.

"Does that make us bad people?" I asked.

"Naw baby, that makes us the people other couples are jealous of."

Thinking back on those events, I can't help but laugh. Dex and I were and still are hopelessly addicted to each other. We've been married for seven years and still can't get enough. I don't mind being whipped by his dick because I know that my pussy has got him in check. Even now that I'm eight months pregnant with our first child he still finds me irresistible.

I can honestly say that I am lucky as hell to have a man like Dexter. He loves, accepts and indulges my oral fetish and I in turn do the same for his. Many people end up having to bury their innermost desires when they settle down. Luckily for me, my man likes to let my freak flag fly. Like Dex says "We're the people other couples are jealous of."

Author's Note

I think the best way to know if a couple is going to last is to look at their sex life. If they have bad communication in the bedroom, they'll have bad communication in other areas of their life together. If they are judgmental and closed minded in the bedroom, they'll be judgmental and closed minded in other aspects of their life together. I'm not saying that sex is the most important part of a relationship but it is one of the most important parts. If the sex is bad then I can guarantee that the couple is not happy.

<u>TURNED OUT</u>

Life is crazy as hell. Moments that seem insignificant at the time can be the most life changing. Those are the moments you look back on and think how the hell did I survive before then?

That's the point I'm at now. My entire life and sense of self changed with one blow job. Naw, it actually changed before then. If I was honest with myself, which I'm getting better at doing these days, I would say my life changed with an instant message. Had I not replied to that message; I would have never met Sonya and in turn I would have never known my true potential as a man.

It takes the right woman to make a man act the right way. Sonya is the right woman for me. Soul mates don't change who you are but rather bring out a side of you that you didn't know existed. Sonya did that for me and I will forever be grateful. So yeah, I'm glad I logged on the internet that rainy Saturday night.

One year ago

April in Chicago was no joke. It could be seventy degrees in the morning and by that same evening snow would be dusting the sidewalks. For that reason, I was spending my rainy Saturday night at home. The last thing I wanted was to end up getting stuck in a storm. Leaning back on my leather sofa, I rolled through my mental index of possible women to call for some company but none of them appealed to me.

It was time to recruit some new pussy. I placed my laptop on my lap and logged on to my favorite website RealFreaks.com. This site had everything I was looking for: fine ass women down for a no strings attached relationship.

I quickly entered my username and password. Fifty new messages, I thought to myself. I wasn't really surprised since I was one of the good looking men on the site. I stood 6'1" tall with a smooth caramel complexion, deep dimples and slanted chocolate eyes. I was a little on the skinny side but that was fine. On this website body weight didn't matter if you were packing and I definitely was.

Bypassing the emails, I went straight to the instant message app. Chances were, if a woman was logged on this late at night, she was in the mood for the same thing I was: sex. Soon after I opened up the app the pings started rolling in.

BBW4Fun: hey sexy

Absolutely not! Nothing wrong with big girls but they weren't exactly for me. I liked my women stacked not fat. Next!

Mlk_Choc_Hottie: ooooweee bb, u r so f!ne.

Naw, she wasn't for me. I liked women who could spell. Next!

FreakLikeMe1100: hey baby.

Now this looked promising. I decided to give it a shot.

LetMeIn2010: 'Sup baby. How are you?

FreakLikeMe1100: Nothing much, just looking for something to do tonight?

LetMeIn2010: Me too. Maybe we can find something to do together.

FreakLikeMe1100: That's cool. How freaky are you?

LetMeIn2010: Very!!

FreakLikeMe1100: Threesomes?

Damn, I had hit the motherfucking jackpot with this one!!

LetMeIn2010: Yeah, I'm into that.

FreakLikeMe1100: Cool because my husband and I swing both ways and have been looking for a man that can handle the both of us. You down?

Aww hell naw!! This bitch had me fucked up. I may have been willing to try a lot of things but I drew the line at messing with another man. I didn't get down like that. I quickly exited the chat and waited.

The night was not looking promising, I kept getting hit on by all types of freaks that either didn't interest me or were too much for me. I was just about to log off and call one of my standbys when that familiar ding sounded from my laptop.

MindFuckMe1st: hello.

LetMeIn2010: hey. How are you tonight?

MindFuckMe1st: I'm well, how are you?

LetMeIn2010: Pretty good. What are you trying to get into?

MindFuckMe1st: Nothing right now, just looking to chat.

Shit, and just when I thought I had a winner.

MindFuckMe1st: but I may be convinced to change those plans.

LetMeIn2010: What can I do to convince you?

MindFuckMe1st: tell me about you and what you're into, sexually?

LetMeIn2010: my name is Kyle. I'm 25, live in Chicago, west side. I work in marketing. I have no kids and no girlfriend. Sexually, I guess I'm into the regular stuff but I'm willing to try anything that is not homosexual or illegal. You?

MindFuckMe1st: I'm Sonya. I'm 23, live in the burbs. I'm in school right now, I want to be a journalist. I have no children and I live on campus.

Sexually, I'm into anything that brings me pleasure…as long as it's legal lol.

For the rest of the night, Sonya and I chatted online and then finally on the phone. She told me that she doesn't meet anyone, male or female, in person without getting to know them first. I could respect that since the internet was full of crazy people. We both decided that we would talk for a while via phone and internet and then meet in person at a public place. If the chemistry was there we would take it to the next level.

Normally, I wouldn't have even wasted my time if the woman wasn't willing to meet a.s.a.p. but there was something about Sonya that drew me in the moment I saw her picture. She wasn't pretty in the typical sense but it was her uniqueness that made her stand out.

She had wide eyes, a slender nose and full lips that reminded me of a peanut butter brown baby doll. Her body looked like it was made for sex. Her 38DD breasts, full hips, thick thighs and a fat ass gave me an instant hard on. Even with all of that, it was her eyes that made me want to wait. Her eyes were almond shaped and the darkest shade of brown I had ever seen on a person. They reminded me of the woods in Minnesota, dark and full of secrets.

I wanted to know all the secrets she possessed and make them mine. I wanted to lose myself in her gaze for endless hours. I wanted to stare into those captivating eyes while I was buried deep inside of her. For that, for Sonya, I'd wait.

Two weeks had passed and I was finally going to meet the spellbinding Sonya. Two weeks of nightly phone conversations, daily texts and the occasional Skype. I looked forward to our chats. Topics ranged from sexual experiences to politics. No matter what we were discussing she always enthralled me. Her soft, melodic voice drew me in like a bear to honey and I wanted to lap it up.

Stepping out the shower, I checked the clock for the umpteenth time. I was anxious, not just for the potential sex but just to be around her. I wanted to spend time in her presence. The feeling of excitement coursing through my veins was new to me. I was never so hard up for a woman, so eager to be around her and deep inside her. I wanted to impress her and make her want me just as much as I wanted her.

So, I pulled out all my tricks of seduction. I got a fresh hair cut that morning and had my beard lined up. Dark wash jeans and a lime green polo shirt complemented my skin tone. All of that combined with extra fresh breath and Issey Miyake cologne ensured that I'd have her senses on overload.

Finally, it was time for me to leave. I quickly slipped into my SUV and gunned it to the suburbs, not caring if the state troopers saw me. The trip from Chicago's west side to Sycamore only took an hour, usually, it would take two. I pulled into the diner's parking lot and checked myself out in the mirror. Damn, I look good. I knew by the end of the night I would have Sonya eating out the palm of my hand and hopefully I'd be eating out her pussy.

The moment I walked into the diner I saw her and our eyes connected. A bright smile lit up Sonya's face and she stood. When she began walking, no, gliding, towards me I broke out into a cold sweat, my head felt heavy, and butterflies buzzed in my stomach. Shit here I was, a grown ass man with butterflies flying around like I was a love starved teenager.

She stopped in front of me and hugged me tight, her lush curves pressed against me and her scent enveloping me. Leaning back, she blessed me with that radiant smile. "Hey, Kyle, it's good to finally meet you in person. I hope the drive wasn't too much."

Clearing my throat, I hoped my voice didn't crack. "No, it was fine and it is wonderful to see you too. You want to take a seat?"

Nodding, she led the way to a table in the corner. After ordering burgers and fries, we talked for a while about current events. I tried to focus on the conversation at hand but my gaze kept drifting downward to her breasts that were definitely on display in her tight tank top. Pebbled nipples pushed against the thin cotton material. I desperately wanted to wrap my mouth around it and suckle like a newborn baby.

Shaking my head, I looked her in the eyes. "I'm sorry, what did you say?"

Licking her full lips, she repeated the question, "What made you join that particular website? It doesn't seem as if you're hard-pressed for women."

"I wanted to meet women who were on the same page as me. I'm not looking for a relationship but I am looking to meet a woman who can match me in bed."

"And you couldn't find that in real life?"

"No, I couldn't. If I met a woman in the club, grocery story or restaurant they would eventually want to move things to the next level. At least on RealFreaks.com everyone knows where they stand and what everyone else is looking for. It's up to you to decide if you're looking for the same thing. What about you?"

She leaned back in her chair, the action pushing her generous chest out further. "I'm not looking for a relationship, though I'm not opposed to it. What I am looking for is someone who is not afraid to explore with me and isn't afraid to try new things. I want someone who can open themselves up to a world of possibilities they never dreamed of. I'm hoping that person is you, if you're down."

Hell yeah, I was down. I wanted her and I wanted her bad. I had been hard the entire night and the thought of feeling those long legs wrapped around my waist was enough to have me ready to cum right in my seat. I told her I was down for anything she wanted to give me, even if it was only her time.

After finishing the meal and paying the bill, I walked her to her late model coupe. Turning to me, she again presented me with that beautiful smile. "Follow me home," she said before getting in her car and turning the engine over.

I quickly hopped in my car and revved the engine up, preparing to follow Sonya to her campus apartment. The ten minute drive felt more like an hour with my blood pressure and dick steadily rising. Finally, we parked and walked up the three floors to her two bedroom apartment. Sonya's dimly lit apartment smelled liked vanilla and lavender, like her. The scent suited her perfectly, sweet, subtly sexy and intoxicating. I took a seat on her sofa and she sat next to me, pressing all of those sweet curves against my side. I wrapped my arms around her and placed her on my lap.

Licking and sucking, Sonya buried her face in the crook of my neck. "You're spending the night."

"Hell yeah," I said, pushing my hands up her shorts. There was no way in hell I was leaving, even if I slept on the couch.

Husky moans floated from red tinted lips into my overheated brain. My fingers tingled as I pushed her tank over her head, grazing the silky hot skin underneath. Large breasts strained against the barely there material of her white bra. Unhooking the front clasp of her bra, I was surprised by the twin silver nipple rings protruding outward.

I gently drew a dusky nipple in my mouth, loving the feel of metal and flesh against my tongue while Sonya gyrated rhythmically against my dick. Hushed swears and heavy gasps left my mouth. Placing a hand in the bend of her back, I gently pulled on her hair to bring her deeper into my mouth. I wanted the texture of her pebbled nipple to be embedded on my tongue but there was another flavor I need to sample.

Laying Sonya back on the couch, I quickly removed her shorts and looked down at her. I had never seen anything as erotic as this caramel beauty laid out in nothing but a thong, wild hair surrounding her face, and nipples as hard as diamonds. I stripped from my clothing and lay between her open thighs. Licking her through the lace of her thong, her moans heated my blood to a boiling point.

After freeing her from the lace confines, I gazed at the prettiest pussy I had ever seen. It was plump, neatly trimmed, wet, and most importantly;

pleasantly fragrant. Nothing ruined a sexual encounter faster than rotten pussy. I bit and licked my way from her inner thighs to her pubic bone and back before diving head first into her succulent waters.

The moment her unique essence landed on my hungry tongue I knew I was hooked. I could tell a lot about a woman from the way her pussy tasted. Sonya ate well, didn't drink a lot and didn't smoke. I could tell all of this just from drinking her up.

I hooked Sonya's legs around my shoulders and gripped her hips tightly, trying to keep her still. I sucked her clit between my lips and hummed, the vibrations making her arch high off the couch. Precum dripped from my rigid dick while her leaky pussy bathed my face in a cum shower.

Spasms plagued her body, her legs held me in a vice grip and my name bounced off the thin walls. I kept up my oral assault until I was certain I had drained her little body. I wanted her to take a minute to recover because I knew that if I slipped inside her drenched walls I'd cum instantly. I didn't need her thinking I was a damn one minute man.

Reluctantly, I pried my mouth from her and looked into her glazed eyes. Yeah, another satisfied customer, I thought to myself. While Sonya came down from her sexual high, I rubbed her body in continuous strokes, familiarizing myself with every curve and valley. Soon, her sighs of content turned into moans of desire and I knew it was time. After turning off the living room lights, we made our way to her bedroom.

"It's a jungle in here," I said and it was.

Her room was decorated in leopard and forest green. A queen sized mahogany bed set smack dab in the middle of the room and was adorned with a leopard bedspread and leaf shaped pillows.

Crawling on the bed, she glanced up at me and shrugged. "I like big cats."

Yeah, I liked big cats too. Chuckling to myself, I joined her on the bed and begin touching her all over. Her skin was so soft, so warm that I couldn't get enough of it against me. With shaky hands I placed on a condom. A moan escaped my lips when I positioned myself between her thighs.

Her faucet of a pussy was again soaking me and I could barely stand it.

My breath caught in my chest when I inched inside her. My arms shook. Her legs tightened around me. Tears left her right eye. My eyes rolled back in my head. This shit felt too good, too right. I've had my share of pussy but this was on another level. Even through the condom I could feel her balmy heat, my thighs were sticky from her pussy's potion, and sweat immediately beaded on my skin.

I could feel the telltale signs of orgasm as I surged in and out, round and round. She matched me stroke for stroke, scratching my back and grabbing my ass. Her soft moans turned into savage groans that triggered my own passionate melody. I had never been very vocal during sex but something about this particular woman had me talking shit, for real.

"You like this shit, girl?"

"Yeah!"

"You want me to stop?"

"Oh God, please don't stop!" she exclaimed while tightening her thighs around me.

"This dick feels good don't it?"

"Yes!"

"Whose pussy is this?"

Looking me in the eyes, she smirked. "Mine."

That fucked up my rhythm and shut me up but I recovered quickly. I opened my mouth to come back at Sonya but the tense pulsating of her pussy prevented me from uttering a coherent word. The clenching was so intense it almost pushed me out of her sweet pussy completely but I hooked those shapely legs on my arms and dove deeper. Liquid fire scalded my dick as she squirted forcefully but I refused to stop.

Leaving the comfort of her pussy temporarily, I pulled her up onto all fours before plunging back inside. I reached for her heavy, swinging tits and pulled on those nipple rings causing her to arch backward. I pulled her hair roughly, making that ass fit snugly against me for deeper penetration.

Repeatedly, I slapped that ass while she threw it back at me. This was the shit I wanted, needed. I needed a woman who can handle my ten inches deep inside her. Sonya reached back and grabbed the back of my neck, placing that fat ass right in my lap. This put her in control of the tempo. Her hips swiveled in short, fast circles.

The feel of her ass in my lap, the relentless clenching of her core, and the fiery liquid scorching my dick brought me to the brink. I tried in vain to resist the inevitable but it was no use. Sonya, like the big cats she loved so much, purred as she came long and hard.

That pushed me over the threshold into orgasmic bliss. Spurts of hot cum shot from the base to the head and filled the condom. I wished that I had known her better because nothing would have been better to release inside her, filling her up.

Orgasmic shudders ripped through our bodies leaving us breathless. Never had I cum so hard with a woman before. That fact left my mind reeling. Not ready to leave her body, I cradled her to my body. Pressing her firmly against me, I licked and nipped the back of her neck until her soft snores lulled me to a peaceful sleep.

"Where you going, you just got home."

"Out," I answered.

I had just gotten home from work and was getting ready to leave again. My older brother Chris, and I shared an apartment and he was always tracking my comings and goings.

"Where?" he asked, taking a seat on my bed.

"I'm going to visit Sonya."

Throwing a pair of socks at my head, he laughed. "Man, that girl got you whipped. You work all week long and instead of going out with your boys, what do you do? You hop in the car and drive two hours to see some female."

"You're just mad because you aren't getting any pussy," I laughed, even though he was telling the truth. For the last two months, I had spent nearly every Saturday night locked inside her and every Sunday morning eating breakfast in bed.

"Yeah, whatever. You just be careful out there."

Chris left the room and I finished getting ready. I couldn't lie. I was super excited about seeing Sonya again. It had been a long seven days and the best way to alleviate the stress was to be locked tight inside a warm body.

No woman had ever made me feel this way. I hadn't even contacted the other girls in my phone who were local but here I was breaking my neck to go out to the middle of nowhere. Why? Because I was pussy whipped.

Two hours later I was sitting in Sonya's living room watching some documentary on television. With her head in my lap, my feet kicked on the coffee table, and a beer in my hand I could feel the tension start to leave my shoulders and neck.

"Kyle?"

I looked down into those pretty brown eyes. "Yeah, baby."

Sitting up, she turned off the television and looked at me. "I want to try something different tonight. You down?"

I nodded and Sonya led me into the jungle. Lying on the bed, I waited for her to show me what she wanted to do. I watched in heated anticipation while she dug in an antique chest at the foot of the bed. Finally, she stood and a blindfold was in her hand.

Breathing became a chore as she straddled my chest and impaired my vision with the satin fabric. She left my body and again I was forced to wait for her next move. The soft clank of metal against metal assaulted my ears followed by the coolness of steel being wrapped around my wrists. Sonya spread my legs wide and tied each foot with a rope, securing the other end to the bed posts.

Feathery kisses trailed down my neck before settling on my chest. Sonya licked, flicked and bit one nipple before moving to the other causing me to arch as high as the restraints would allow. I couldn't stop the litany of moans that poured from my lips.

Usually I was the one suckling nipples, not the other way around. Sonya drew a path to my navel, dipping her tongue in and out, driving me insane. I hoped, no, wished, she would put that pretty mouth on my dick and suck me into oblivion.

Unfortunately, she had other plans. My ankles, calves and the indention of my knees were her focus. I reacted instantly, my erection hardened to a painful point, my breathing became labored and a light sheen formed on my body. I feared I would cum before I even received head.

She sucked and kissed up one thigh than the other before running her fingernails lightly against the moist skin. I relaxed into the bed when suddenly she put me in her mouth. No, she didn't just put me in but she swallowed me whole, forcing me down her open throat. I knew instinctively that this blowjob was a life changer.

Sonya's strong jaws clenched and released repeatedly. Her fingertips caressed my balls in delicate strokes. Her head bobbed up and down, placing me in and out of the confines of her hot throat until I damn near cried. I wanted desperately to run my fingers through her silky hair, to watch her please me but the handcuffs and blindfold prevented it.

Every one of my senses that wasn't impaired was heightened beyond belief. I could smell the intoxicating perfume of lavender, vanilla, and aroused pussy. I could feel the cold of the handcuffs against my wrist, the roughness of the ropes around my ankles and the silky heat of Sonya's mouth wrapped around me. I could hear the slurping sounds she made and the pounding of blood in my ears.

Everything was intensified including the orgasm that was about to erupt in my loins. A strangled yelp left my lips and my hips pulled deep into the mattress when Sonya bit the head of my dick.

"Did I tell you to cum yet?" she asked calmly.

I wanted to call her a crazy bitch and tell her to untie me but some secret part of me liked this game we were playing. Even though I was scared, all I could do was whisper, "No."

I felt her body leave mine and, again, I was forced to wait. Minutes ticked by and I wondered if she had forgot about me when I heard her reenter the room. Once more, she quickly made my dick disappear in her throat. My hips bucked and I fought with everything inside me not to cum.

The scent of peppermint wafted into my nostrils seconds before a tingling shot up from my balls to the tip of my dick, swelling it. Every suck, every stroke, and every pull became more exaggerated. Moments before I came she removed her mouth.

An icy jolt tore a scream from my throat. She had filled her mouth with ice water and began sucking my balls. The sensation of the cold water combined with her hot mouth sent me into overdrive.

My head thrashed about on the bed. My arms pulled at the handcuffs. I heard Sonya swallow deeply and chuckle. Hot sauce, warm water and more peppermint oil had me climbing up the walls but it was what she did next that sent me spiraling.

Cool air repeatedly floated over my balls from Sonya's parted lips. Her sure hands and lips worked in unison to relax me. I had pretty much melted into the cotton sheets when I felt her part my ass cheeks. Automatically, I tensed up, but her soft voice floated up to me calming my fears. Her insistent licking and biting made me more aroused. Confidently, she licked my asshole and stroked my dick. The new feeling of a tongue stroking my ass and the feeling of her gripping my dick tightly was too much to bear.

"I'm cumming!!"

Swiftly, she released the blindfold before pushing me deep in her mouth. I watched in ecstasy as she greedily drank every drop from me. Sonya continued to milk me relentlessly, sending me headfirst into another orgasm.

Back to back orgasms and a severe case of aftershocks had my mind swimming. Shaky gasps were released from my heaving lungs while Sonya freed me from my confinements.

Snuggling next to me, Sonya ran her hands up and down my chest. "You okay, baby?"

Soft whimpers were my only response. *If my homies could see me now*, I thought to myself.

She chuckled. "It's okay, baby, I understand. That was new to you."

"Hell yeah, it was. I've never had a blowjob like that and I certainly never had anybody do anything to my ass." I pulled her closer to me. "You're a real freak, huh?"

"Yeah, I am. I told you I wanted to explore new possibilities."

"Yeah, you did. So, what other things do you want to try?"

"That depends…how do you feel about other people joining?"

That question gave me pause. If she had said other women I would have been down but she said other people. I didn't want another man anywhere near her, let alone inside her. I also didn't want to seem as if she had me under her thumb. So, I did what I always did when women gave me an impossible question. I lied. "Shit, baby, I don't mind at all."

Pulling the blankets on top of us, she gave me a sly smile. "I thought you would say that."

As I watched her sleep I was filled to the brim with sense of foreboding. I knew that Sonya wouldn't hesitate to call my bluff. I just hoped that when that day came I wouldn't land my ass in jail for another man touching my woman. My woman. Yeah, my woman. I liked Sonya a lot, a hell of a lot to be honest. I would do whatever it took to make her mine.

Earlier in the day I had gotten a text from Sonya telling me she had a surprise for me and to meet her at seven. I was excited and a little nervous. I was excited to see her, to get between those creamy thighs, and to cum in her mouth. I was nervous because it had been a month since I told her I didn't mind other people joining us and that had yet to happen. A part of me wanted to take it back and demand that she be with me and only me but when it came to Sonya I was happy to let her be in charge.

I was truly submissive with her which definitely was a first. I had always been the dominant, the aggressor with the women in my past. It was funny but I actually felt more like a man when she had me bound to her bed or chair. At work, with my family, with my friends I was always in control. It was nice to give up that control and let another person take over.

At seven on the dot, I met her at the designated place. We were to meet in a small town outside of Chicago. In between two cornfields sat a dilapidated looking barn. Cars lined each sided of the long dirt driveway and the street. R&B music with a booming baseline could be heard coming from the covered windows.

Butterflies occupied my stomach as I watched Sonya walk towards me. Though the August night was warm, she was draped in a long black trench coat. We greeted each other with a warm embrace and walked up the driveway.

Sonya knocked on the door four times and it opened slowly. The scene before me made my jaw drop. People in various stages of undress were performing sexual acts in a large room. I looked at Sonya with a question in my eyes.

Leaning close to me ear, she whispered, "It's a swinger's party. I thought you'd like it since you don't mind others joining us."

Before I could say anything she dropped her coat. There was my woman dressed in a fishnet body stocking, black stiletto heels and no undergarments. A chain connected both nipple rings like a leash. As soon as her coat hit the floor; a tall, blond woman grabbed her hand and led her to a couch in the corner.

All I could do was follow. I watched in heated silence as the blond fondled my woman while I rebuffed the advances of other women. I witnessed the glazing of my woman's eyes, the glistening of my woman's pussy and the beading of my woman's nipples as another woman kissed and caressed her.

My traitorous body hardened immediately and I silently cursed. This was what I had thought I wanted, my woman and another woman enjoying each other, but now I wasn't so sure.
Swearing softly, I yanked Sonya off the sofa, grabbed her coat off the floor and pulled her outside. "Put this coat on. I'll meet you at your house. We need to talk," I said before storming to my car and slamming the door.

Thirty minutes later I was pacing her living room floor while she calmly sipped an apple martini, still wearing that body stocking. "Why are you so mad?"

"Are you serious right now?" I fumed, even though I was asking myself the same question.

"Yes, I'm serious. Explain to me why you're upset."

"I don't want anyone else touching you," I said softly.

"But you told me that you were okay with it."

"I know."

"So, you lied?"

"Yes," I mumbled.

She licked the sugar off the rim of her glass and stood. "Follow me."

Seconds after I had entered the jungle, I was tied to the bed with a blindfold over my eyes. Goosebumps formed on my skin as I heard her digging through the chest.

Expectation coiled through my body, I knew what was coming. I knew that at any second she would put that pretty mouth on me and take me to heaven. Sonya dragged something long and cold up over my feet to my chest. The object sliced through the air before landing across my nipples with a loud whap.

"What the fuck?" I screamed, trying to free myself.

"I don't like liars, Kyle."

WHAP!! The belt came down again against my nipples. It was hard enough to sting but gentle enough not to cause any real damage.

"Liars have to be punished." Two more lashes punctuated her meaning. "You embarrassed me tonight and that cannot be tolerated. Do I make myself clear?"

She hit me two more times before I hissed, "Yes."

"Yes, what?"

"Yes, Sonya."

She rained three more blows, making my nipples raw and sore. "Yes, what?"

I knew what she wanted. I guess subconsciously I had always known. Succumbing fully, I whispered, "Yes, Mistress."

"Good boy."

I was rewarded for my submission with the release of the blindfold and more strokes of the belt. With each whip I felt myself become more aroused. My dick hardened worse than ever before. My heart beat furiously in my chest. Tormented moans of pleasure flew from lips. I felt weak and strong at the same time. I loved every second of it. The smug smile on Sonya's face let me know that she realized the effect she was having on me, had always had on me.

Suddenly, the sweet torture stopped and I looked in her eyes. Sonya crawled up my body, that body stocking showing everything yet oddly concealing at the same time. Her hot pussy was above my mouth and I would give anything to taste it, not that I really had a choice.

She tore the crotch of the stocking and looked at me. "You're going to lick my sweet pussy. You're going to push your tongue deep inside it and then you're going to suck my clit. If you do it wrong or if you bite me I will punish you."

"Yes, Mistress," I said right before her pussy lowered on to my face.

I dove straight in, moaning hard. She smelled so good, tasted so delicious and I knew I would kill another person trying to cop a taste. This was my big cat.

Every time I got really into it she would remove her pussy from my hungry lips. I knew if I begged she wouldn't concede but if I waited patiently she would reward me with more of her sugary nectar. I tongued her g-spot, sucked her clit and licked her folds expertly until she bathed me in her juices, shuddering on my tongue.

She dragged her body towards my dick, leaving a trail of sticky wetness in her wake. I watched as she turned around, wrapped me in a condom, and mounted my dick. I was a little disappointed because I wouldn't see her face while she came but then again I did have a front row seat to that fantastic ass.

All thoughts left me when I felt her slick walls engulf me. I bit my lips to keep from screaming loud enough for the neighbors to hear. I knew then that Sonya Ballard owned me, mind, body, heart and soul, and I wouldn't have it any other way.

I melted into a pile of whimpers and tears while she bounced up and down on me, her thick cream covering my dick. She looked back at me and gave me a haughty smile. "You okay, Kyle?"

All I could do was nod and moan like a little bitch. Sonya's legs locked against mine and her body corkscrewed harder and faster. Her back arched and she brought me deeper inside. Large patches of caramel flesh were visible through the holes in the stocking. The ends of her long hair danced across my thighs. That feeling alone made me want to cum.

The indicative pulsating of her sugar walls began and her hips moved faster. My hips surged forward, desperately trying to help her reach the ultimate high. Her high pitched screams filled the air and her body convulsed.

Slowly, she did a circle on my dick, coming to face me. The look in her eyes told me all I needed to know. With a loud roar, I gave in to the scorching orgasm I had been holding back since she whipped me. Hot cream filled the condom to bursting as I came multiple times. Hot air seeped from my mouth as Sonya gently licked my sore nipples before she took me from her body and released me from the restraints.

She disappeared into the bathroom before coming back to clean me up. Afterwards, she pulled me into her arms and I laid my head on her generous breasts, feeling content.

"You okay, Kyle?"

"Yes," I whispered, the hot air from the words causing her nipples to bead up.

"I'm glad. I need to discuss a few ground rules with you," pausing, she kissed me on the forehead and I snuggled closer. "One, you will always refer to me as Mistress when we are home but in public I will be Sonya. Two, you will never lie or embarrass me again. Three, you belong to me and you will follow my commands without hesitation or trepidation. You will know that I would never do anything to hurt. Anything I decide is for your own good and pleasure."

I agreed as a sense of acceptance and serenity overflowed in my body.

"I never want you to feel ashamed or less than about our relationship. In a Dom/sub relationship the sub has the strength. It takes a strong person to give up control to another. To trust another person to make decisions for them, take care of them and love them. Know that I will always put your wellbeing first and in turn you will put my happiness before your own."

Present Day

From that day to now, I have felt nothing but happiness and peace from belonging to Sonya. Every time I think she has brought me to the limits of sexual pleasure she proves me wrong. Whips, paddles, fuck machines, you name it we've tried and I have always enjoyed it. I derive gratification from knowing that I am a good sub to her and I know that I will make a great husband as well.

Last month, Sonya proposed to me by slipping my engagement ring in her pussy and making me eat it out. I think I'm the only man I know who has an engagement ring but I don't care. I know it took a lot of courage for her to ask me and I would have never dreamed of saying no.

In fact, if I was honest with myself, like I said, I'm getting better at that, then I would have to admit I wouldn't have dreamed a lot of the things that have happened this last year. I couldn't imagine falling in love with one woman. I couldn't envision spending my life with that woman. I certainly couldn't have dreamed of being turned out the way I had but shit, life's a crazy thing.

With one blowjob, my fate was sealed and I forever belonged to Sonya. Had I not logged on to

Realfreaks.com that rainy April night, a part of me would have never been fulfilled. I would have never known my true potential as a lover and a man. Sonya has done that for me. She made me realize that a man's true potential is not measured with the amount of woman he has bedded but how well he satisfies the one that means the most to him.

"Kyle."

"Yes?"

"Come to bed."

"Yes, Mistress."

Author's Note

Many assume that in BDSM relationships the man is the Dominant/Master and the woman is the sub/slave. In all actuality, many men are the sub/slave. Not because they are weak but because they are strong enough to realize that real manliness comes not from a machismo façade but from accepting who you really are.

<u>RAVEN</u>

When I looked in the mirror, I could honestly say I loved what I saw on the surface. At 29 years old I, Raven Smith, was a beautiful woman. I was 5'8" with a hazelnut complexion, long black hair, and light brown eyes. My body was tight and right with small breasts and slim hips. I was often asked if I was supermodel which of course I didn't mind.

I had it all. I lived in one of the most prominent suburbs of Chicago, had a closet as big as some apartments, filled with every designer known to man, a successful interior design company I owned with my sisters, and parents that loved me. Yeah, I had it all but I was unbelievably miserable. Why? Because my husband Dean was not who I thought he was.

If you knew Sparrow, my baby sister, you had probably heard her say a million times that my husband was a drug dealer and I was a dumb ass for not realizing it. That was absolutely ridiculous. I had been with Dean since I was fifteen. Fourteen years I had been with this man, married for ten, so I knew exactly what he did. Shit, who gave him the money to start moving pounds? That was me.

My daddy, Jay Bird, made sure that all of his children had access to money. While my sisters, Sparrow and Robin, and my brother Blue, spent their money on material things I helped my man come up. Why didn't I help him get a job or go to college? Well, because Dean had assured me that it would be a temporary thing.

One thing he didn't tell me was that it was easier getting in the game then getting out. The money and the power were more addictive than the drugs. Honey, if I knew then what I knew now, I would have wasted my money at the mall with my siblings instead of on a man.

Looking in the mirror, I couldn't help but ask myself how the daughter of a prominent African-American family could end up married to one of Chicago's biggest drug kingpins? That was an easy answer, I was a dumb ass!

At the tender age of fifteen I decided to get closer to "my people" and took my dumb ass to the south side. One of my girl's cousins was throwing a party so, I lied to my parents and went. I walked in and laid eyes on Dean.

He was breathtakingly handsome even back then. The first thing I noticed was that he was one of the few men I had to look up at with my heels on. Standing at 6'7", the color of warm honey, dark chocolate eyes and deep dimples, Dean commanded the attention of every woman in the place. Luckily, or unfortunately, depending on how you looked at it, he only had eyes for me. By the end of the night I was sitting on his lap feeling like the luckiest girl in the world.

Fast forward fourteen years and I felt as if my luck had run out. Dean was cheating on me. I didn't have proof but I knew he was. A woman knows when her man was cheating. It was like women came built with a bullshit detector and mine was beeping so loudly it was a wonder that I could even think clearly.

It was the little inconsistencies that kept me on alert. He was staying out later, claiming that he was working. Yeah, right. All of sudden you had to work late? He started working out. I had been trying to get him to workout with me for the last two years and all of a sudden he realized that his slight beer belly wasn't cute? I didn't think so. Shit like this had the hairs on the back of my neck standing up and my Spidey senses tingling. Something wasn't right.

Kelis's Milkshake bounced off the bathroom walls. Without looking at the caller id I knew it was Sparrow. I debated on whether to answer then hit the talk button. "What up?"

"Nothing much boo, what are you doing?"

"Staring at this beautiful girl…oh wait it's me in the mirror," I said chuckling.

"Ewwww…you know you're as ugly as homemade sin."

"Whatever Sparrow, you wished you looked this good," I said, running a hand down my flat stomach. "What do you want?"

"Damn, I can't call to say hello." I waited for her to get to the real reason for the call. "Okay, I'm calling to let you know about this dude I just met."

Rolling my eyes, I left the bathroom and flopped on my bed. Sparrow was the world's biggest slut and she was proud of it. She actually bragged about having a stable of hoes. Those were some punk ass dudes if you asked me. They all knew about each other and yet didn't mind. She had just got rid of this dude Sean and now she was on to the next one.

"Earth to Raven, did you hear me?"

"Yeah, I heard you. What about this guy?" I would have lectured her about her promiscuity but she wouldn't have listened anyways. With Sparrow it was best to just let her do what she wanted. Plus, lecturing was Robin's job.

"His name is Isaiah and he is fine as fuck!! We met at the gym. He purposely chose the treadmill next to mine even though there were many others available. We exchanged numbers and I'll probably call him tomorrow."

"Why not wait until he calls you?"

Sucking her teeth, she said, "Because I want to establish from the beginning that our contact will be on my terms. You can't let these men think that you'll follow wherever they'll take you. You have to show that you have some control over the situation or you'll end up miserable."

Amen, I thought. I let Sparrow finish telling me about this new guy and the rest of the hoes while trying to keep my opinions to myself. It wasn't like I had room to talk. People in glass houses shouldn't throw stones. If anyone's house was glass right about now it was mine and I knew that eventually it would all come crashing down around me.

The stench of weed, stale liquor and body odor assaulted my nostrils as soon as I stepped into the hole-in-the-wall club on the city's west side. This definitely wasn't the type of place I'd usually frequent, but then again I wasn't there for pleasure. I was looking for my husband.

Looking around the club, I found his trifling ass back in the corner surrounded by his goons and some ratchet looking bitches. Dean's ass was so busy grinning up in some hoe's face that he didn't notice me. But his right hand man Piccolo did. And from the widening of his eyes, he knew all hell was about to break loose.

Now, normally I behaved in the classy manner my mother instilled in me. I never raised my voice at my husband, nor did I interfere with his business. I always tried to be calm and rational and speak with him in a dignified manner. But sometimes a woman had to pull her clown suit out and let her man know she wasn't one to be fucked with.

Tonight was that night for me. That was why I tracked his ass down, drove forty minutes into the city and was standing there shooting daggers at him with my eyes at two in the morning. Lifting my head high, I stormed across the room towards Dean and his crew. Before I could make it halfway, Piccolo grabbed my arm and pulled me away.

As soon as we were outside I snatched my arm from him. "Fuck is your problem P?" I hissed.

"Not here, Ray. You can't do this shit here."

"This doesn't concern you," I said, looking into his hazel eyes.

"That's where you're wrong sexy," he said, pausing to light a cigarette. "If you go inside there and cause a scene you'll affect business. Nigga's will start clowning D's ass and thinking he's a joke. When niggas think you're a joke, that's when they want to fuck with you. This means I have to start busting skulls around here. I'm not down for that shit."

"Last time I checked that was your job, Piccolo. If you're not happy with it why don't you leave?"

His harsh laugh made me flinch. "Aww Princess, you still haven't learned have you? You don't get to leave this shit; the money and the power are too intoxicating. Now you baby, you can leave any time you want," he said softly.

Silently we stared at each other. The orange glow from the street light hit Piccolo at an angle, making him look like a bronze statue. His hazel eyes glittered like marbles as they perused my frame. I'd be a fool to say I wasn't attracted to him. He was just as tall as Dean, had the same complexion and dressed in the same manner. However, it was his quiet strength and his subtle gentleness that drew me.

Unconsciously I leaned into him and lifted my head. My lips begged to be kissed by him. I wanted to feel his strength, needed to absorb it. I was so close I could feel the heat from his body and his breath against my face.

Wrapping his fingers around my neck, he drew my head closer to his. A moan escaped my parted lips as he rubbed his nose along my jaw line up to my ear. "Go home Raven," he whispered before releasing me and gently pushing me away.

He leaned against the building, watching as I got into my white on white Range Rover. Grudgingly, I started the engine and pulled away from the curb. I was in no hurry to get home to be alone in my cold bed. I would have gone to one of my sister's homes but I was in no mood for them. Sparrow was probably entertaining one of her many men and Robin was probably counting down the days until she reached menopause.

Twenty minutes later I reached our condo in the Loop. I could've made the trip back to our home in Plainfield but I didn't want to make the drive with so much on my mind. Piccolo and I had almost made a grave mistake. Fortunately, he had enough sense for the both of us.

Dean only asked two things of me: honesty and loyalty. Wasn't that ironic? The two things he commanded from me were the same things he refused to give. Piccolo and I both knew the consequences for being disloyal to Dean was death. Well, at least for Piccolo. Dean wouldn't kill me. He'd beat my ass, disfigure me, but he wouldn't kill me.

Walking into my fifteenth floor condo, I set my Birkin bag on the marble end table. I picked up the remote and depressed a button. The wall length drapes lifted and the illuminated sites of the Loop were before me. I had been to Paris, New York, Japan and Los Angeles, but there was nothing like Chicago when it was lit up.

Stepping out of my silver Prada heels, I let my pedicured toes sink into the lush white carpet. I picked up my babies and walked into my private closet to put them away in their original box. I stripped out of my skin tight jeans and blouse and made my way to the shower.

As I waited for the steam to fill the bathroom, I piled my hair on top of my head and removed my makeup. Stepping into the shower, I finally allowed my emotions to be free.
I was angry at Dean's lack of respect towards me, fed up with his infidelity and sickened that I had allowed myself to be in this situation; but mostly I was bursting with a deep sense of longing. I was twenty-nine years old, married and surrounded by a loving family yet I always felt alone.

Closing my eyes, I willed the hot water to rinse away my worries and loneliness. Images of Piccolo's handsome face flashed before my mind's eye. Instinctively, my nipples hardened, breath caught in my chest and my pussy throbbed. Of their own accord, my hands caressed the twin peaks into painful points.

"Can I help you with that?"

A scream lodged in my throat when I quickly turned and realized it was Dean. He stripped from his expensive suit and joined me in the shower. He didn't bother to wait for my response since I never denied him anything he wanted. Maybe that's the problem. All thoughts fled my mind when I felt his hot mouth encase my nipple. Closing my eyes, I let him give me the pleasure I needed.

Pushing my small breasts together, he pulled my nipples into his mouth, sucking until I moaned earnestly. Kneeling in front of me, he kissed my pubic bone before diving deeply into my sensual waters. Dean's mile long tongue stroked and tasted everything from my clit to the crack of my ass. I writhed uncontrollably on his face, silently pleading that he wouldn't stop. He continued his oral assault until he was licking cream from his chin and my body was slumped against the shower wall.

Gathering me in his arms, I wrapped my long legs around his narrow waist. Dean roughly pulled my hair back, forcing me to look him in his eyes. His eyes said everything I needed to know, I had better not come looking for him again. As usual I conceded to his demands.

Gripping my thighs tightly, he plunged deeply inside me. Groans escaped both of our lips. No matter how hard he acted, my pussy always brought Dean to his knees. This pussy was his and his alone. I had never let another person so much as look at it and he knew it.

We worked our hips against each other, trying to wring pleasure from one another. The sounds of water hitting the marble, skin slapping skin and melodious moans created a sensual symphony that I couldn't handle. Reaching down, I firmly cupped his balls. His hips pumped into me harder and faster signaling his orgasm. My walls clenched around him repeatedly, milking him for everything he had. We came together. My name was screamed from his lips while my heart screamed Piccolo's.

"I do believe our baby sister is in love."

Glancing at Robin from behind my dark Ray Bans, I smirked. We had just left Sparrow's house and were now driving down the expressway towards Chicago for some shopping. "Girl please, Sparrow doesn't know how to love."

"That's not true. Everyone knows how to love Ray. And if she doesn't maybe Isaiah can teach her."

I rolled my eyes at the skyscrapers outside my window. "You're forever the romantic, Robin. Doesn't that ever get tiring?" I asked.

Robin was always the one to believe in soul mates and true love. I didn't believe in shit like that. I believed that you met someone, developed feelings and worked at making a life together. If it worked then great, but if it didn't you moved on to the next person.

"No, it doesn't. There is someone out there for everyone," she said.

"You think this guy Isaiah is 'the one' for Sparrow? I don't. I think he's just another notch in her belt," I grumbled, folding my arms across my chest.

"What's wrong, Ray?" Robin asked me.

I considered lying just so she would stay the fuck up out of my business but I knew that she wouldn't leave it alone until I came clean. "I think Dean's cheating."

"Aww, for real."

"What's that supposed to mean?" I asked, turning completely in my seat to stare at her profile.

Sighing, she hesitated briefly before answering, "Raven, Dean's been cheating on you for years. I thought you knew so that's why I never mentioned it."

"Why didn't you say something to me?"

"Every time either Sparrow or I would mention Dean you would cut us off. You would say, 'I know what my husband is and what he does, so you bitches can mind your own business.' After a while we got tired of trying to tell you. Seriously though Raven, you cannot sit here and say that you didn't know. He's just like Daddy, sloppy as hell."

Wiping the tears from my eyes, I finally admitted to myself what I had known all along, Dean was cheating on me. The evidence had always been there but I chose to ignore it. Piccolo's words came back to me. 'You can leave whenever you want.' Was that what I wanted? Did I want to leave my husband? Did I want to start over all by myself?

Turning back in my seat I again focused on the scenery whizzing past. I didn't have the answer to any of those questions but I knew I needed them soon. There was no way I could continue to live in quiet misery with a man who didn't truly love or respect me and I wasn't sure if I even loved or respected him anymore.

Yeah I had some shit I needed to figure out, but the real question was whether or not Dean would let me go.

Two months had passed since I had left Dean. We weren't officially divorced or separated but we were taking a break. I needed him to see that I was serious about not taking anymore of his shit. I kept the house in Plainfield while he stayed in the condo.

From what I heard he hadn't been using our time apart to evaluate our marriage. In fact, he was having hoes over to the condo every night. That made me angry. Here I was keeping my body clean for him and he was out with dirty bitches every night. Sparrow told me I needed to go out and meet someone new and finally I was taking her advice.

I had received an invitation to an art gallery opening on Chicago's north side and I planned to make my debut as a semi-single lady. I dressed in a cream colored turtleneck sweater mini-dress, a wide chocolate belt and chocolate over the knee Alexander Wang boots. Chocolate pearls draped down my chest and matching earrings adorned my ears. The last thing for me to do was the hardest. Raising my left hand, I slipped the three carat ring off my third finger on my left hand and set it in my jewelry box.

Thirty minutes later, I arrived at the gallery and gave the valet my keys. Stepping inside, I was greeted by the low hum of those discussing art, negotiating prices or just trying to be seen. Beautiful portraits, landscapes and abstracts hung on snow white walls and easels, illuminated by strategically placed lighting. I moved across the polished oak floor from one painting to the next, keeping a mental note of which ones I wanted while sipping champagne.

"What's a beautiful woman like you doing here alone?" asked a deep, velvety voice behind me.

Turning around, my breath caught in my chest. "Piccolo?"

Placing my shaking hand in the bend of his elbow, he leaned down and whispered, "In the flesh, baby girl. But around these parts you can call me by my birth name, Pierre."

"I didn't know Piccolo wasn't your real name," I said as we passed by paintings and patrons.

He paused and faced me. Staring into my eyes, he placed a wayward lock behind my ear.

"There are a lot of things you don't know about me, Raven."

"What are you doing here? Did Dean send you to check up on me?" My defenses were up. A man like him didn't attend events like these without a purpose.

"Don't flatter yourself, baby. Dean doesn't even know I'm here. The artist is a friend of mine and I came to support. I saw you standing there looking sexy as always and decided to keep you company."

"So, Dean has nothing to do with this?"

Piccolo's...Pierre's...whoever's grip on my arm tightened as he pulled me into a secluded corner. The dim lights created shadows across his face, making him appear even more handsome.

He gently pushed me against the wall and placed his hands on either side of my face. Leaning closer, he pressed his upper body against mine until he was the only thing in my line of sight. The fabric of his lightweight wool suit brushed against my exposed skin and caused me to shiver with excitement.

"Let's get something straight sweetness, Dean doesn't control me. In fact, in the next few months that name will be a distant memory."

"What does that…"

"I wasn't finished." Waiting until I was quiet, he continued, "Right now, I'm getting my shit together but what I want you to know is that you are definitely on that list."

"Oh." My heart was pounding so furiously I was certain he could feel it through his suit jacket.

"Since the day I met you there's been this connection."

I wouldn't deny that.

"That nigga Dean doesn't deserve you."

I wouldn't deny that either.

"I'm not asking you to divorce him and marry me. All I am asking Raven is to let me show you a world of possibilities. Let me show you a world where instead of your control being stripped from you, it will be your choice to give it freely."

As quickly as he had appeared he was gone. The loss of his body heat and his words sent a chill through me. Piccolo had done what Dean had never been able to do, mind fuck me.

There was a fine line between manipulation and mind fucking. Dean manipulated me. He used my naiveté to mold me into what he wanted me to be, give him what he needed and to achieve the success he desperately wanted. He did all of this by eradicating me of my control, self-esteem, and voice.

Piccolo…Pierre mind fucked me. As I looked back, it was obvious he had been doing that from the start. He had used his quiet strength to draw me in and leave me wanting for more. Without touching me, he made me ache with desire with his caressing gazes, soft spoken words and gentle demeanor. He encouraged me to be better, calmed me when things didn't go my way and protected me when the shit hit the fan.

Dean tried to force his way into my head and dominate it. Pierre patiently waited for me to let him in and once I did, he didn't try to dominate the space that he occupied with me. Yeah, I was mind fucked and God help me, my body wanted to be next.

Taking my phone out of my clutch, I called the only person I knew could help me. "Sparrow, can I come over?"

"Yeah, Ray, I'll be here."

Forty minutes later I was sitting in Sparrow's living room, relaxing on her sofa in front of the fire. I had just told her about the events leading up to tonight, the confrontation at the club, the conversation with Robin and the encounter at the gallery.

"So…what do you think BB?" I asked her, calling her by her childhood nickname.

One thing about our family, we were all named after birds. My father, Jay Bird, my mother Tianna "T" Bird, my older sister Robin Bird, me, Raven Bird (now Smith), Sparrow Bird and our brother Blue Bird. Growing up, everyone called Sparrow Baby Bird since she was the youngest out of us girls and she always hated it.

"Don't call me that!" she said with exasperation. "First off, you were really sloppy out in front of the club. Dean could have caught the both of you at any time and you both would have been dead. Second, we all know that Dean's a cheating motherfucker. I saw him around town once with some popped looking hoe and told him that if he was ever out in public with another bitch and I heard about it, I would chop his dick off and shove it up his ass."

"You're always so eloquent, Sparrow."

"Third, if I were you I'd fuck the shit out of Piccolo...Pierre. That man has had it bad for you since the day he became Dean's business partner."

Gazing into the fire, I whispered, "Can I tell you something Sparrow and you promise not to tell anyone?"

"Yeah, Ray."

"Dean's not a business executive." Pausing, I took a deep swallow of my wine. "He's a drug dealer."

"No shit, Sherlock," she stated sarcastically.

Ignoring her interruption, I told her everything I had kept to myself over the years. I told her how we had met, how I financed his first big lick, how I stashed the drugs for him and created a false company for him. I told her how Piccolo/Pierre wasn't a business partner but Dean's right hand man and enforcer. I told her how I wanted to leave Dean but I was afraid I'd never be free from him. By the time I was done spilling my soul and unleashing my demons Sparrow was wearing a shocked expression.

"Raven, what the fuck have you gotten yourself into?" she whispered with tears in her eyes.

"I've been asking myself that question for a long time. Honestly, at the time I thought that it would only be temporary. He had me so wrapped up in him and his lies that I would have done anything he asked of me."

Handing me a Kleenex, Sparrow asked the question I had been asking myself for the last two months, "And now?"

"Now I realize that he was just using me. Now that he doesn't need me or my money, I'm just a trophy on his arm." I paused to gather my thoughts. "I'm ready to leave my husband," I sobbed, crumpling into a weeping pile of heartache in my baby sister's arms.

"You look tired, baby."

Glancing up, I smiled at Pierre. Today was our first "date" and I was nervous. After leaving Sparrow's house two weeks ago I officially filed for divorce from Dean. I thought he would come to me and demand to work it out, but the joke was on me. I hadn't heard from him at all.

In fact, the only person I heard from besides my family, was Pierre. I didn't tell him that I was divorcing Dean, but I did accept his invitation to share a meal. Pushing the thoughts from my mind, I focused on the man in front of me.

"It's been a long couple of weeks."

"Yeah, I heard."

Raising a brow, I leaned across the small table towards him. "What exactly did you hear?"

"For starters, I heard about Sparrow. How is she?"

"She's as well as can be expected."

Three days after my emotional breakdown in her living room, Sparrow's house was set on fire.

The police and fire department were both investigating. Personally, I believed an angry ex-hoe of hers was to blame.

"If she needs anything let me know. I also heard about you and Dean."

Scrutinizing the snowy scenery outside the Italian eatery's window, I whispered, "I filed for divorce. I just couldn't do it anymore."

"Raven, look at me, I'm not going to sit here and say I'm sorry because I'm not. I always thought you could do better than him. You deserve more than to be a kingpin's wife."

"Really? So, what makes you so different than Dean? I mean, you're hands aren't exactly squeaky clean are they?"

Leaning back, he crossed his arms across his broad chest. Hazel eyes glittered in admiration. "I like this new you, it's about time you started speaking your mind."

"Answer the question."

"We have more in common than you think. You probably assumed I was some gangster who only wanted quick money and lots of power. You also probably assumed that I never had any type of ambitions or culture. Don't try to deny it, I saw the way you looked at me at the gallery opening."

"I won't deny it." I couldn't deny it. The first thoughts to run through my mind were what was he doing here and did Dean send him.

"I grew up in the suburbs just like you, though not as affluent. My mom is a realtor and when the market dropped my mom lost her job. We went from an income of ninety thousand a year to twenty-five. My dad had left us a long time ago; so it was up to me to be the man of the house. I refused to let my mom lose what she had worked so hard to obtain and a job at McDonald's wasn't going to make up a sixty thousand dollar deficit."

"So, you started dealing."

"Yep, but I wasn't cut out for it. Then Dean saw me one day at the local gym beating the hell out of a punching bag. You both had just gotten married and he was looking for someone to help protect you. At the time the streets were crazy. Niggas was fighting over every single block and he didn't want his new wife to become a target. So, he brought me on.

It's always been temporary in mind. I had dreams of going to college and making my mom proud. I'm not saying that I'm not grateful for Dean, because believe me I am. Thanks to him, my mom's house is paid off and I put all three of my younger brothers through college. But...I've given that nigga ten years of my life and I refuse to give him anymore."

I stared at him in amazement. It was as if we were both freeing ourselves from the golden shackles and marble prison Dean had provided us. I told him as much.

"Exactly. That's why I've been taking online courses for the last four years to get my degree. I plan on going into business for myself in the IT sector. There isn't shit I can't do with a computer." Pausing to take a sip of his soda, he smiled at me. "So Miss Raven, what do you think?"

His smile was infectious and I found myself returning it. "I think that we do indeed have a lot in common."

Weeks had passed since my first date with Pierre and I wanted him in my bed so bad I could taste it. Oddly, I didn't feel bad about wanting to fuck him so soon after we started dating. It was as if he had been courting me for the last ten years and we were now ready to consummate the relationship. Tonight we were celebrating the turn in our relationship and the fact that he had finally graduated.

When I pulled up in front of his house in Sycamore, I was definitely surprised that Pierre lived in a beautiful single family home in the suburbs. I had always expected him to live in an apartment in the middle of city. I guess being involved in what he was involved in, it was easier to maintain your sanity away from the action.

I was in for more surprises when I stepped inside. Polished wood floors, toasted almond walls and original artwork gave the foyer the warmth that my home lacked. As I walked further into the house, my mouth continued to hang open. Most men who lived by themselves had homes that lacked sophistication and charm. Pierre's didn't have that issue.

Sitting in the dining room across from Pierre, it was obvious that I was in disbelief. As part owner of an interior design company, I was used to being in beautifully decorated homes but his surpassed all that I have seen. I told him as much.

"Thank you. That means a lot coming from you," he said, blushing.

"I truly mean it. My home is nothing compared to yours."

"Baby, I've been to your home and it is stunning. You have Italian marble covering almost every square inch, antique furniture and beautiful artwork."

Spearing another shrimp, I savored the succulent flavor before stating what I thought was the obvious, "True but your home was noticeably designed with comfort and family in mind. My home was created with one purpose, to show the world how much success Dean had achieved." Swallowing hard, I looked at him. "Just like everything else in his life."

Without saying a word he crossed the table and lifted me out of my dining chair. He held my hand, drawing circles on my palm, as he led me to the sunken living room. Sitting down on the overstuffed sofa, he placed me in his lap so I was straddling him, my leather skirt rising.

I expected him to run his hands up my bare thighs, to make my blood boil with lust, to take my mouth in a heated kiss. I expected everything and anything but what he gave me.

"Let it out Raven." The extreme tenderness in his voice, the gentle strokes on my back, and the feeling of contentment was all too much for me.

On a shaky sigh I released all my anguish, insecurities and shame on to his sturdy chest. Heart wrenching sobs racked my body but Pierre kept stroking me, holding me and encouraging me to let it out. As my cries slowed to sniffles I felt like a weight had been lifted off of my shoulders. I looked up at Pierre and was rewarded with a smile that illuminated the dark corners of my damaged soul.

I reached up and traced the outline of his full lips with trembling fingers. A strangled moan poured from my throat when my finger disappeared in his hot mouth. I had never thought of my fingers as an erogenous zone and I had never seen anything as erotic as my long, slender digit encased between his full lips, being bathed by his tongue. Until now, until Pierre. We stared at each other while he continued to suckle me.

Releasing me, he buried his face in my chest, whispering, "Take what you want, Raven. Tonight is your night to take back your control."

I gently pushed his head back until he was resting against the back of the couch. Confidently I rose up from his lap and took off my clothes. Silk and leather fluttered to the carpeted floor leaving me clad in a sheer purple bra and panty set, black stockings, garters and stilettos.

Pierre's breathing changed, coming in short and shallow gasps. A shiver passed through him so quickly that if I had not been watching him intently I would have missed it. Knowing that I could make this powerful man tremble boosted my self-esteem and made me aware of my sensual potency. Turning on my heel, I heard his sharp intake of breath as I presented him with my perfect heart shaped ass.

Without sparing him a glance, I made my way to his bedroom and sat on his mahogany dresser, crossing my long legs. Browns, reds and gold created a masculine environment which suited the situation. I wanted to be the only feminine element in his space tonight.

Pierre entered the room and stood before me, head bent and hands in his pockets. Light perspiration mingled with my tear stains causing his shirt to cling to his muscular body. His submissive stance triggered a surge of dominance to flow from my pounding heart to my quaking pussy. The feeling was intoxicating, hypnotizing, addicting.

"Look at me," I whispered.

Lust filled hazel eyes collided with supremacy filled light brown ones.

"Undress."

Without hesitation he began unbuttoning his shirt. Glimpses of honeyed skin over granite muscles came into view. Never taking his eyes from me his hands moved to his belt buckle. My heavy breathing and the clanking of his belt followed by the rasp of his zipper were the only audible sounds in the room. The moment his erection was freed from its cotton restraints; my heart thudded in my chest and my mouth felt as dry as the desert.

Having a naked Pierre standing in front of me caused my brain to overheat and my new found confidence to plummet. Biting my lip, I was hit with a moment of indecision. What did a woman do when a beautiful man was waiting naked in front of her?

"Do whatever you want, sweetness," he said as if he read my mind.

"Lay on the bed."

An idea materialized out of nowhere. I disappeared momentarily into his closet before returning to stand next to his California king bed. Pierre's eyes flickered to the items in my hand and a slow, appreciative smile played on his lips.

I straddled his middle, cradling his dick between my thighs, and tied each hand and foot to the bed post with four silk ties before blindfolding him with another. Only after he was securely bound and his vision blocked did I finally remove the rest of my clothing.

Kneeling over his calves, I moaned as his hot skin touched mine. Settling between his legs, I lightly ran my nails up and down his inner thighs causing him to flinch. Cool air rushed from my pursed lips. Lust induced sweat dripped from my forehead, evaporating as soon as it touched his fevered body.

Flicking my tongue out, I trailed it from his knee to pelvis, relishing the flavor that was uniquely Pierre. I licked, sucked and bit my way up past his washboard abs, hair dusted chest and broad shoulders before arriving at his full lips.

Those lips! Those lips had brought me so much pleasure over the last couple of weeks but I had saved one for tonight. Placing each leg on either side of his head I knelt over his face. Pierre pulled on the ties as the heat from my overly aroused pussy fanned his face, the scent driving him insane. I waited patiently until he settled down. Slowly, I lowered myself inch by inch towards his face. My slick lips met his full ones and a groan of satisfaction bubbled from his throat into the walls of my pussy.

Gripping the headboard tightly, I rotated my hips in time with the strokes of his tongue. It flowed effortlessly from the base of my pussy to the top, diving deep, stroking my g-spot and suckling my clit hungrily. Lightning bolts of erotic pleasure shot up from the soles of my feet to the top of my head before settling deep in my sugar walls.

Animalistic howls teemed from my raspy throat as I came but I refused to let him taste my creamy goodness. Quickly, I removed myself from his face and slipped his beautifully curved dick into my awaiting mouth.

He tasted of heaven, decadence, strength, vulnerability, love and home. I became drunk from the taste and the feel. I felt every buck of his hips, every pulse of his veins and every pound of his heart in my soul.

Tearing my swollen lips from Pierre's swollen member I prepared myself for the ride of my life. Dean never let me ride. He always had to be in control. Pushing Dean and his negativity from my mind, I ran the head of Pierre's dick against my swollen folds.

Shudders of anticipation ran through the both of us. As much as I enjoyed dominating him I knew I had to get Pierre inside me now or I would incinerate. Rising above him, I slowly encased him in my tight body.

"SHIT, RAVEN!!" Pierre screamed once he was fully embedded in me.

"Mmm, did you say something?" I asked cockily while I bounced on top of him. I was truly feeling myself.

"It's so fucking good. Baby, untie me please. I need to touch you."

I refused to answer him. This was my night and I was going to do what I damned well pleased. Deciding to grant him a miniscule amount of mercy, I leaned over and took the tie off of his eyes.

Staring back at me were eyes filled with so much lust, desire and longing that I almost came on the spot. Up and down I rode, clenching my pussy on the upstroke and relaxing on the downward, all the while maintaining eye contact.

That feeling was coming over me. I could feel the fire and ice rushing through my veins and my heart was racing to explosion. Pierre's dick swelled inside me, almost to bursting. His face twisted in pleasurable pain. His hips bucked harder.

My hips corkscrewed faster. Sweat covered his face. Sweat trickled down between my breasts. His breaths came in pants. My breaths came in gasps. My name flew from his lips and his from mine. Cum spurted from his dick into my waiting core. I squirted my passion for him, soaking the bed.

Limply, I freed his hands and feet from their bounds before collapsing on his chest. Still connected, he trailed his fingers over my spine until I fell asleep. It wasn't until I woke up the next morning that I realized I had forgotten the condom.

"Oh, so you're on that Rihanna shit now?"

"Fuck you, Sparrow!" I laughed.

Two weeks after my romp with Pierre, my sisters and I had gathered at Sparrow's home to help her get settled back into her house. The restoration company had finally gotten the house back into a livable condition just in time for Christmas. Unfortunately, the arsonist was still at large.

"I'm saying though, you had that man tied to the bed. It was like a verse out of her song S&M."

"Real funny." Glancing at Robin, I waited for her to join in the conversation but she continued to go through a box of books as if it held all of life's secrets. Glancing at Sparrow, I silently mouthed, "What's wrong with her?" She shrugged.

"Um, Robin, how's it going over there?" asked Sparrow.

"Fine," she replied, still not looking at us.

Stopping in front of Robin, I knelt down to her level. It was then that I noticed the dark smudges under her eyes, unkempt nails, faded and stained clothing and barely combed hair. Robin, always the professional, was put together at all times. Even if she was going to the grocery store she made sure she looked like she had just stepped off the cover of Black Enterprise.

"What's wrong Robin?"

"At what point in your life do you finally start playing by your own rules?"
Sparrow, of course, was the first to answer, "As soon as you start breathing. Shit, I've always played by my own rules."

"That's why we're here Sparrow," I said, waving my hand around the room. "Because you played by your own rules without any thought to other's feelings. Maybe if you were more like me…"

"Bitch, please."

"And actually considered the feelings of others before doing what you wanted, then you wouldn't have some psycho running around town burning your shit down. No, what Robin needs to do is live her own life but be respectful of others."

"So, I guess you were being respectful of Dean, your husband, when you were fucking his best friend."

"Fuck you, Sparrow!!"

"HEY!" screamed Robin. "This was about me but since you want to make it about you let me tell you both what I think. Sparrow, you are in no position to tell anybody anything right now. You have somebody stalking you, trying to physically harm you and you have yet to tell your boyfriend about your past.

Now, Raven. You are a married woman. Yes, you filed for divorce but you are still married. Out of all the men in the world you could be fucking; you chose your soon-to-be ex-husband's best friend and business partner. That's foul as hell. Both of y'all are in no position to give anybody advice that's why I didn't want to ask you. So, can we please get back to doing what we came here to do so I can go home?"

Silently, we all got back to the tasks at hand. My mind was racing a mile a minute. It wasn't as if I didn't know that my relationship with Pierre was foul but it was different to hear it from Robin's lips.

Maybe subconsciously I was trying to hurt Dean but deep in my heart I didn't think so. I was developing deep feelings for Pierre. If my sisters thought things were bad now I could just imagine how they'd react if I told them I thought I was pregnant.

If there was one place I hated most in the world it was hospitals. The smell, the food, the décor, I hated it all. It's funny how you didn't notice those types of things when an emergency hit. As I raced down the corridors of the hospital towards the nurse's station, it was as if all five senses had suddenly left me.

"My name is Raven Bird, my boyfriend was admitted."

Before the nurse could give me any information, I heard my name. Turning, I saw Pierre's mother and brothers waiting in a small room. "What happened?"

His mother tried to speak but only sobs came out, not a good sign. Pierre's brother, Samuel, finally was able to find his voice, "It was a freak accident. He was driving down the street when a semi rear-ended him. They were at a red light and the semi just decided not to stop."

A chill ran up my spine. I mindlessly sat in the chair nearest me while Samuel continued to speak. I couldn't hear a word he was saying. "Huh? I'm sorry."

"P's fine. I swear an angel was watching him. He only broke his collarbone. We can all go back to see him in a few."

We sat in silence and waited to be notified by the doctor on Pierre's condition. We all knew that it would be awhile. It was just after the holidays and people were lined up in the hospital. Everyone was trying to fulfill their New Year's resolutions and most of them ended up injuring themselves in the process.

A few hours passed before the doctor appeared. "Raven Bird, Mr. Lester would like to see you, alone."

I hugged Ms. Lester and went to see my man. I was pleasantly surprised to see that he was only hooked up to a few machines and that he was awake. His face was bruised from where it collided with the steering wheel. His neck was covered in heavy bandages. All in all, he was still gorgeous.

Waiting for the doctor to leave, he motioned for me to come closer. "Raven, I need you to do something for me."

Taking his hand in mine, I kissed his knuckles. "Anything."

"I need you to go to the house. There's a safe in my room with one hundred thousand dollars in it. I need you to get my mom and brothers on the next flight to Georgia. I have a house down there. The keys are in the safe. The combination is your birthday. Then I want you to go to your parents' house and stay there until I tell you. Okay?"

"Okay, but why? It was a freak accident. Shit like this happens all the time."

"Naw Raven, there wasn't anything accidental about this shit here." Pausing, he squeezed my hand. "That nigga Dean is trying to kill me."

I returned to my home in Plainfield well after two in the morning. I showered and slipped between the sheets on my bed. It took forever to get Pierre's family to agree to head down to Georgia without giving them any specifics. It took even longer to get them packed and on the airplane.

I called my sisters and let them know what was going on. Sparrow was a wreck but with her own issues she couldn't be of any assistance. Robin offered to let me stay with her but with her mood swings I knew I couldn't handle that shit. So, I told my parents that my house was being fumigated and I needed to stay with them for a while.

I couldn't wait for my man to give me the word to come back to him because staying with my parents was going to send me to the nut house for sure. Until then, all I could do was dream of having Pierre with me, holding me as I fell fast asleep.

Hours later, sunlight radiated through the curtains covering my bedroom windows. I yawned deeply and I stretched my arms over my head. The silk sheets slipped beneath my breasts. I wished that Pierre was there to give me some of that morning loving I had grown accustomed to. His scent was still embedded in my sheets and that drove my desire to a higher level. I thought about finding him and riding him into the sunset but changed my mind. I would do what he asked and lay low until he told me to come out.

Opening my eyes, all I saw was the darkness of the barrel of a 38. Special aimed between my eyes.

"Good morning Raven, Daddy's home."

DEAN!

Author's Note

If you've read my book Running then you've already met Raven in the story Sparrow. That just leaves their older sister's Robin's, story to tell and believe me that is one story you don't want to miss.

RED DOOR

Late at night, if you drive forty-five minutes from the city of Chicago and down Heroin Highway; you'll find a small town where big dreams can come true. Dreams so taboo, so forbidden, people would pay an insane amount of money to keep them buried.

Welcome to Red Door where our motto is, "We'll treat you right…For a price." There is nothing, and I mean nothing, we won't do to keep our customers happy. We believe that everyone's fantasies should come true as long as they're legal.

You won't find us in the yellow pages, on the internet or in a magazine but we are well known amongst Illinois' elite. An invitation to Red Door is better than gold dipped pearls wrapped in silk inside a Maserati. Pearls can be lost and a Maserati can be damaged but a night of mind-numbing, insanely gratifying sexual encounters cannot be lost or damaged but will forever remain in your memory.

Don't think it's worth the hefty price tag? Well, allow me to convince you. Three of our members, the politician, the musician and the school teacher, can all vouch for Red Door.

The Politician

Illinois is plagued by political scandal. Corruption runs through the bloodstream of our political system like water through a stream. I have been in the public service sector for most of my life and have been publicly serving Illinois for five years.

Who am I? You can call me Tom. As a member of this system I have the obligatory doting wife, the smart kids and the big house in the suburbs. On the outside life looks picturesque but on the inside, tensions were brewing.

My wife and I have shared a bed for our twenty plus year marriage but rarely have sex. She is cold and unfeeling. She doesn't want to try anything new. Sex is for procreation and release not for pleasure. I can't blame her, not really. If anyone was to blame; it is her shrew of a mother.

My mother-in-law had repeatedly told my wife while growing up that sex was dirty and "good girls" only did it for the purpose of having children. I knew all of this when I married her and despite that, I thought I could change her views. I failed miserably.

Don't get me wrong. I love my wife. I can't imagine being with anyone else but I have needs. Actually, I have a fetish. I was at the point of divorcing her and dealing with the professional consequences later; when an invitation to Red Door floated across my desk. I had heard about it but thought it was a myth. Thankfully, it wasn't. From the moment I landed on the doorstep of Red Door I felt an inner peace.

The first person I met at Red Door was Danni, the owner. She took one look at me and knew exactly what I wanted. "You're a furry," she stated nonchalantly.

"Yes," I said with shamed filled eyes.

I had been interested in being a furry for years but had never found the courage to act upon the impulse. A furry was a person who liked to have sex while dressed as a stuffed animal. The costumes are never taken off and only animal noises are verbalized which makes the possibility of recognition slim.

Reaching across the desk, Danni took both of my large hands in her slim ones. "There is nothing to be ashamed of. As long as it fulfills you and it's legal we can help you."

Danni took out a pamphlet that outlined the company's mission and pricing packages. Package one allowed the client to visit three times a year and satisfy any fantasy of their choice for $10,000. Package two allowed the client to visit four times a year for $15,000. Package three allowed the client to visit six times a year for $20,000. Finally, package four allowed an unlimited number of visits for $100,000. Without hesitation I picked and paid for package four.

"Great, now we have a few rules here at Red Door. Number one, you will always call before you come here. We need ample time to set up your fantasy unless you just want to have random sex with someone here. Number two, you will use our provided transportation to escort you here and back to the location we choose. Number three, and most importantly, if you divulge any information about Red Door, our practices or any employees; your membership will not only be terminated but there will be severe consequences."

I wanted to tell her that she need not worry about me disclosing any information. Any inkling of my sexual fetish would be political suicide. The people of Illinois might forgive politicians for bribing, misappropriating funds and perjury but they would definitely rebel at the hint of sexual deviancy. Without a moment's hesitation I signed the contract and left Danni's office.

Three weeks later, I finally had my first fantasy appointment at Red Door. I waited at a large mall in the suburbs for my transportation. A nondescript minivan pulled in front of me and a pretty blond rolled down the window. "Get in, Tom."

I did as I was told and hopped in the backseat. We rode through the back roads of the suburbs to our destination as I discreetly checked out my driver. She was about 5'5" with the skin the color of warmed cream. She had bright red hair that fell into ringlets around her shoulders. She wore a short black skirt and a bright green top that brought out the color of her emerald eyes.

"What's your name?" I asked her.

"Pilar," she said, looking at me through the rearview mirror.

"What do you do for the company?"

"Whatever needs to be done," she answered vaguely. "Look, why don't you sit back and relax, we'll be there shortly."

Taking the hint, I leaned against the seat and closed my eyes. My body hummed in anticipation.

I was finally going to bring my fantasy to life. I prayed it would be everything that I hoped for. I was paying a lot of money and risking not only my political future but my family life to gain sexual completion.

Soon, we arrived at Red Door. The building was a large brownstone in a suburb located off I-88, also known as the Heroin Highway because a suburbanite could take the highway straight to Chicago's west side to score heroin. The grounds of the company were neatly manicured and potted flowers lined the sidewalk and driveway but it was the bright red door that gave the sex club its name.

Pilar drove us to the front door and I quickly got out. Per instruction, I knocked on the heavy door once, twice, then four times. The door opened slowly and an older gentleman stood before me.

"Yes?" I showed him my membership card and he stepped aside. "Stay here while I get Danni."

I took a seat on an antique chair in the foyer. Once again, I marveled at the elegance of Red Door. When one thought about sex clubs they didn't think about antiques, chandeliers or Persian rugs. My reverie was stopped when I heard the clicking of heels against marble floors.

I watched as Danni approached me. She was an attractive woman. Danni was 5'9", had generous breasts, wide hips and an ample ass. Her skin reminded me of chocolate pearls and her hair was in an asymmetrical cut that brought out the angles of her heart shaped face.

Stopping right in front of me, she held out her hand. "Nice to see you again, Tom. What's in the bag?"

Taking her hand in mine, I replied, "Nice seeing you again as well and it's my costume." She nodded and led me down a long hallway. "Here's how it works with furries. Since the furry experience is a group experience there is a mixture of my people and some clients. Everyone must wear their costumes at all times." We stopped in front of a large door. "Here you are. You can change in this room and a connecting door will lead you to the party. Have fun."

I stepped inside the large changing room and stripped. I put my clothes and personal belongings in one of the wooden lockers and locked it before stepping inside my panther costume. A panther was perfect for me. It was everything I wanted to be in my real life, sleek, sly and confident. I made sure all flaps were in place and eyed the red door leading to the party. Before I could change my mind, I hurriedly opened the door leading to paradise.

Animalistic noises, the scent of linens mingled with arousal and the sight of costumed figures greeted me as I entered the room. No beds were in the room but plush carpeting covered the space. Mirrors lined the walls and dim gold lighting bathed the space. Foliage was sporadically placed about, giving the space a jungle or forest feel.

I stood in a darkened corner observing the activity when a lioness approached me, her breasts protruding in the tight costume. The seat of her costume was darkened with moisture and the scent drove me to confusion. She rubbed her body against mine before softly roaring in my ear. No words were spoken as animals couldn't talk. I rubbed my paws along her curves and was rewarded with a deep purr.

I pulled her closer to me and leaned against a mirrored wall while she worked her round ass in the seat of my costume. My dick stood proud against the flap and a loud growl bubbled from my chest.

I wrapped my paws around Ms. Kitty's breasts as she gyrated against me. She twirled and swiveled those hips against me while I watched the other patrons. A cheetah and bear were grinding across from the lioness and I. A dog and an armadillo were rubbing on each other, while a naughty cow was pleasing herself in the middle of the room. Other animals were scattered about, each lost in their own sexual pleasure. Roars, purrs, growls, moos and even chirps could be heard over my own heavy breathing.

I laid Lioness on the ground and placed myself on top of her to begin yiffing. Yiffing was what I had always dreamed of doing but until now I couldn't see it as a reality. To grope, fondle and reach climax without penetration was the ultimate goal for a furry, my ultimate goal.

I wrapped her legs around my waist and rotated my pulsating erection against her hot spot. She purred repeatedly in my ear, driving me wild. I pumped against her, pawed her breasts and nuzzled her until she came long and hard. I moved her to doggy style position and continued my assault.

Animal sounds left my lips as I moved against her, watching the actions in the mirror. I saw a hen approaching us but I refused to stop. The hen wrapped her wings around me and grinded her hips in my ass making the lioness beneath me mewl in intense pleasure.

This was more than I could have hoped for, two women yiffing me at the same time. Lioness and Hen switched positions and I repeated my movements causing Hen to chirp wildly. I felt orgasm loom over me and I tried to fight it. I lay on the ground and motioned for both ladies to take me to another world. I wanted to see something that you would never see in the wild, a hen and a lion pleasing a panther.

My dick throbbed inside the sweat soaked costume and howls and growls released from my throat. I watched Lioness and Hen paw each other while continuously humping me. Cum spurted from my over stimulated dick, drenching the confines of the costume. Hen and Lioness lay on either side of me, stroking me, nuzzling me as I came down from my sexual high. I stayed there for long moments afterward, listening to the others as they reached fulfillment before I finally got up.

I changed my clothes and left the changing room. Pilar was waiting outside the door for me, sitting in a chair. Her long legs were crossed and her thighs were exposed by her short skirt. I walked towards her and fondled her small breasts, watching the nipples pebble as her head fell back.

Silently, I led her back into the changing room and put on a condom. I dove in and out of her soaking pussy, pounding her relentlessly. My blunt nails nipped her sensitive thighs. My anxious mouth found her long throat and left my mark, I was feeling territorial. She threw that pussy at me and I bit my lip to keep from cumming, it was inevitable.

Her screams vibrated through my dick making me climax. I pulled out of her dripping center and she took off the condom, catching the cum in her mouth. She made a show of swallowing every drop and I pinched her nipples in response.

We arranged our clothes and left the room. Easy silence engulfed us on the ride back to the mall. When we reached our destination, she parked in a secluded area of the parking lot. I kissed her deeply and fingered her until she came again against my fingers. Releasing her, I hopped inside my luxury sedan and whistled all the way home.

The Musician

I had only visited Illinois a couple of times before I heard of Red Door. I usually would stop in the city for a tour and press then leave the next morning. Who am I? You can call me Peter. I want to make it very clear that I have never, nor will I ever, be hard up for women. Shit, I have been an R&B artist for over fifteen years for crying out loud!

The fact of the matter is; when you're in the public eye there are certain things you cannot do. Having group sex with younger women is one of those. Now don't get me wrong, I'm not a pedophile. I like my women between the ages of eighteen and twenty-one.

However, young women are not known for keeping secrets especially when a star is involved. So, it definitely was a blessing when I received an invitation to Red Door in the mail to my home. A home no one knew anything about. At first I was skeptical but my curiosity got the best of me and I called to set up a consultation with Danni, the owner.

I met up with Danni at my private home in the hills of L.A. I was immediately attracted to her though I knew she was not in my preferred age range. Before I could open my mouth she voiced my innermost feelings. "So, Peter, you like younger women."

It wasn't a question but I felt the need to answer anyways. "Yes."

"May I ask why?"

"Shit, baby, I've been asking myself that for a long time. I guess the only explanation is that they don't get any ideas of marriage or commitment. Most of the time, they are just happy to be with a star. Their bodies are tight in all the right places and they are willing to learn what pleases a man."

I must have said the right thing because she nodded and slid a pamphlet in front of me. My eyes nearly popped out of the sockets when I saw the prices.

"Before you get worked up about the prices Peter, let me explain what you'll get in return. Not only are you paying for your fantasies, no matter what they are, to be fulfilled but you are also paying for discretion. Every woman you sleep with is on my payroll and they are tested regularly." Pausing, she leaned forward, giving me a tantalizing glimpse of her breasts. "Though each girl is trained in the art of pleasing a man they are willing to learn your specific likes and thoroughly enjoy sex."

"I'll take package three."

"You won't regret it."

"I'm sure I won't," I said, smiling.

"Great, now we have a few rules we need to go over. Number one, you will always call before you come to Red Door. We need ample time to set up your fantasy unless you just want to have random sex with someone there. Number two, you will use our provided transportation to escort you there and back to the location we choose. Number three, and most importantly, if you divulge any information about Red Door, our practices, or any employees your membership will not only be terminated but there will be severe consequences."

I agreed and went to my safe to take out $20,000 cash. There was no way I was going to break any rules and either be physically harmed or involved in a scandal with the black Heidi Fliess. Stuffing the cash in a Louis Vuitton backpack, I tossed it in her lap and told her I'd see her in five weeks.

Five long weeks later, I was sitting in the back of a minivan on my way to Red Door. A member of Danni's team, Trina, had picked me up from a sandwich shop on Chicago's south side. I leaned my head back against the seat and tried to relax.

I only had one night in town under the radar. Tomorrow, I'd be expected to hit the stage and give thousands of fans a show they would never forget. Tonight, I was hoping to get a round of sex I would never forget.

An hour later, we pulled up in front of a brownstone with a big red door. "So, that's why you call it Red Door."

"Ah, beauty and brains…It's a wonder you're not taken," Trina sarcastically stated.

I decided to ignore her caustic comment and knocked on the heavy door, once, twice, then four times. A man answered and I showed him my card. He pointed to a chair and I took a seat, silently marveling at my surroundings.

I didn't know what I was expecting but it certainly wasn't what I saw. Elegance and sophistication surrounded me, putting me at ease. The sound of heels hitting marble floated into my ears. Danni was slowly approaching me, a smile on her beautiful face. Instantly my dick hardened.

She motioned for me to stand and placed my hand in hers. We walked down a long corridor, strange sounds emitting from one of the rooms. "Is that mooing?"

"Peter your room is here on the left. If you need anything let me know, I'll be in my office upstairs."

I watched her walk back down the hall, my eyes glued to her perky ass. Shaking my head, I opened the door that would lead to my fantasies. Blue and purple lights bounced off the walls and were reflected off the mirrored ceiling. A bar lined one wall and a huge circular bed sat in the middle of the room. The bed was covered in black silk sheets and throw pillows. Fluffy white carpeting surrounded the bed and lit vanilla candles were placed sporadically around the room.

Three ladies, all dressed casually in t-shirts and skirts, sat at the bar sipping on colorful drinks. Their soft giggles and shy glances propelled me further into the space.

"How are you ladies doing tonight?" I asked, taking a seat on a barstool.

"Good," they answered in unison, setting off another round of giggles.

"What are your names? How old are you?"

"I'm Jasmine and I'm 19," answered the first girl. Jasmine was tall, around 5'9", a caramel beauty, her Latin heritage apparent. She had small breasts and a big ass. Her dark wavy hair reached the crack of her pert ass and I wanted to run my fingers through it.

"I'm Sarah and I'm 20." Sarah was the oldest with a smooth chocolate complexion and almond shaped brown eyes. She was 5'5" and definitely stacked. I wanted to bury my face in her abundant breasts while letting her ass overflow in my hands.

"I'm Tammy and I'm 18," answered the petite Asian on the end. Tammy was 5'3" with a butterscotch complexion. Her body was slender and arousing, small perky breasts, narrow waist, and little hips that my hands could grip for hours.

"Nice to meet you all, will you join me on the bed?" I asked, taking two bottles of champagne with me.

Without hesitation, they followed me to the bed that could easily fit six comfortably. We leaned back, resting our heads on the velvet headboard and chatted for a while. I wanted them to be comfortable before I stripped them naked. As the conversation and liquor flowed, the ladies loosened up. Excited laughter, secret touches and meaningful glances bounced between the four of us.

"Have you ever been together before?" They all shook their heads. "Been with women before?" Again, they shook their heads. "Why don't you give it a try? Aww, don't be shy. I'll tell you exactly what to do." I made myself more comfortable and prepared for the show.

"Jasmine, you kiss Tammy while Sarah and I undress each other."

I kept one eye on the kissing beauties, watching their tongues swirl, while setting free the breasts I wanted to lose myself in the moment I saw them. Engorged nipples stared back me and I lowered my head.

Hershey kisses melted on my tongue and three sets of moans caressed my ears. I glanced to Tammy and Jasmine and realized they were already topless, licking and kissing on each other. Give a group of horny women some liquor and they were bound to try anything.

By the time we were all undressed, I had Sarah on all fours and her head in Jasmine's dripping pussy. Tammy was behind me palming my nipples, driving me insane. I pumped vigorously into Sarah's tight pussy. I watched as she tongued and kissed Jasmine's center hungrily before turning my head to deeply kiss Tammy.

Sarah's high-pitched moans combined with Jasmine's husky groans caused my dick to harden even more. The tightening of Sarah's core, Tammy's small hands on my sensitized nipples and Jasmine's continuous moans had me ready to climax.

Quickly, I pulled out and lay back on the bed. I motioned for the three ladies to come over to me. "That was good. Right now, I need some head."

No sooner than words left my mouth did I have three sets of lips caressing my dick. That image would forever be burned in my mind. Tammy and Sarah sucked on the head while Jasmine lapped at my balls. Ten mind-numbing minutes later, I reached into the bowl of condoms next to the bed before donning one and placing Tammy on top of me.

I gently settled Jasmine onto my thirsty tongue while she and Sarah kissed and fondled each other. I gripped Jasmine's full hips and placed a finger in her ass, her frantic movements and deeps moans were my reward.

I knew that if I wanted I could tap into her virgin ass but decided to save that for another time. I felt the telltale signs of Tammy's orgasm approaching and bucked my hips furiously. Her melodic screams filled the air along with Sarah's, who rode the orgasm on Jasmine's fingers.

Prying the ladies off of me, I discarded the old condom and reapplied a new one. My body was humming with desire and I knew I wanted to cum buried deep inside the Latina beauty, Jasmine. She hypnotized me from the moment I came inside the room. If I had met her any other way I would have tried to keep her with me.

Knowing that wasn't to be, I spread her creamy thighs out on the bed and placed my body on top of hers, I wanted to look in her eyes. The other two women could disappear for all I cared.

Gently kissing Jasmine's lips, I tweaked each nipple. I nipped and bit down the length of her body, pausing to pay attention to her breasts and navel. Finally, I reached her swollen pussy that was dripping with arousal, her fragrance surrounding me. Greedily, I sucked her clit until her juices soaked my face. Sliding up her body, I placed each leg on my shoulder. I could vaguely hear Tammy and Sarah moaning and giggling but my focus was on Jasmine.

I slipped in between her hot folds and nearly climaxed. Her hips matched me stroke for stroke, her nails dug into my sweaty skin and her eyes rolled into the back of her head. My hips corkscrewed into her pulsating body. My hands tightly gripped her hips. My veins bulged in my neck and screams poured from my throat. Jasmine's groans and moans turned into one harmonious orgasmic song that sent my mind spiraling.

"Usted me hace sentirme tan bien," Jasmine screamed, her pussy opening like a flower.

I knew I was making her feel good. I was fucking her better than I had any woman in a long time. My actions did not go unrewarded. Cries of pleasure bubbled from Jasmine's throat as she squirted her ecstasy all over me.

"Aww, fuck," I shouted, quickly pulling out of her leaking pussy.

Like a porno flick, each girl kneeled in front of me and lapped up my pleasure. I watched through lust filled eyes as they kissed each other deeply. We rested for a while, each needing to catch our breaths before we got dressed. I lightly gave each girl a peck before watching them leave, except Jasmine. I held her back from the others.

"What's your number?" I asked while rubbing her ass.

Leaning forward, she whispered in my ear, "I can't tell you. Not because I don't want to, but because it's against the rules."

Not used to taking no for an answer, I pressed the issue. "But I want to see you again."

"You can but it has to be here."

"So, I'm not worth breaking the rules for?" I asked angrily.

She sighed. "Look, Danni's done a lot for me and I respect that. I have a good thing going here. I work when I want, I'm never broke and I'm able to have a life outside of here. Can you understand that?"

Relenting, I set her away from me. "Sure but just know that next time I'm tapping that tight ass of yours."

I walked her out the room and found Trina waiting for me by the front door. We got back into the minivan and headed to the city. Red Door was everything I had hoped for and much more. My body was still humming. I knew that if given the option I'd head back there and get all up in the spicy Latina's ass again.

"So, you like tapping asses, huh?" Trina asked, cutting into my thoughts. Looking out the window, I realized we were almost to the sandwich shop.

Since there was no sense in lying, I told her the truth. "Yeah, I do. Why?"

"No reason, just making conversation," she said, averting her eyes in the rearview mirror. I knew that look on a woman. She wanted to experience what I had to offer.

Reaching the sandwich shop, we got out of the minivan. I took that moment to really look at her. Trina looked about 27, stood 5'7 and she had a honey complexion, average breasts and stripper ass. Her face was stunning with brown baby doll eyes, full lips and a slender nose.

I pulled Trina closer to me and fondled her ass. She halfheartedly resisted me but eventually gave in. I turned her around and pressed her against the car while fishing a condom out of my pocket. Sheathing myself, I lifted up her short skirt and stared in appreciation.

I rubbed my hands repeatedly over the brown globes before separating them. Slowly and gently I probed her asshole until I was fully inside. Trina pushed that ass against me in hard strokes and I met her just as forcefully.

"Shit, baby, work my ass," she screamed, turning me on even more.

This was what I liked about more mature women. They knew how to give a man what he wanted, what he needed. They knew how to make that ass work and bring a man to his knees. Trina knew exactly what she was doing as she tossed her hair out of her eyes and looked at me. I came so hard that my knees buckled and I fell against her, crushing her clit against the car and setting off her own orgasm.

We quickly dressed and kissed each other goodnight. As I drove back to my downtown hotel I thought back on the two women who made this day memorable, Jasmine with her tight, young body and Trina with her sexy, expertise. Before laying my head down, I knew I had to formulate a plan to get those two away from Danni and with me.

The School Teacher

Sometimes life can just suck everything out of you. Between my fiancé, my mother and my boss I was losing my mind. I have been with my fiancé, Myra, for three years and for three years she has taken every ounce of fortitude from me. Combine that with my overbearing mother and my emasculating boss and you have a damaged man.

Who am I? You can call me Stan. All I want out of life is to teach my students, have a family and live in peace. Can I do that? Not if those three harpies can help it. When I received the invitation to Red Door it was just in time.

I met Danni, the owner, at a coffee shop and she was able to tell what I needed. "You need to regain your confidence."

"You have no idea. The only question I have is, will Red Door be able to help me?"

"Yes, we will. In fact, I know exactly what you want." She took my hands into hers. "You want to be able to control someone else, to make them feel pain while bringing them pleasure, you want to reaffirm your position as a man. In short, you want BDSM."

It was incredible the way she could read me like a book. I had been watching BDSM porn, read articles and trolled chat lines. I wanted it but knew that Myra would never go for it. "Yes, I want to try it."

Sliding a pamphlet my way, she waited for me to browse the contents. Some of these prices were three year's salary but I wasn't worried. My grandfather had left me a sizeable inheritance that my fiancé knew nothing about. I had dumped it into a savings account and let the interest pile up until I could figure out what to do with it. Now, I knew exactly what I wanted to do, I wanted to get my confidence back.

"I'll take package two, please."

"Nice choice. Now, we have a few rules we need to go over. Number one, you will always call before you come to Red Door. We need ample time to set up your fantasy unless you just want to have random sex with someone there. Number two, you will use our provided transportation to escort you there and back to the location we choose. Number three, and most importantly, if you divulge any information about Red Door, our practices, or any employees your membership will not only be terminated but there will be severe consequences."

Pulling out my phone, I transferred $15,000 to Danni's account. "You don't have to worry about me breaking any of your rules. I always like to plan time away from my fiancé well in advance. I understand the need for provided transportation and I will never tell a soul about Red Door." Pausing, I looked her in her eyes. "By the way, how did I get an invitation to Red Door?"

"I'll let you in on a little secret and this is strictly confidential. All of our clients are by special invitation only. After being a customer for three years you can then ask for an invitation to be sent to someone you think needs our services. Careful consideration is involved because you only get one invite every three years. After a background investigation is done on the prospective invitee we then have an invitation sent."

"So, that's how you know what I wanted?" I didn't know if I should be angry or happy as hell that someone had thought to invite me.

Giggling, she leaned back in her chair. "Yes but don't tell anyone. It'll ruin my mystique. Clients think that I can look at them and magically know what they want. Anyways, please give me a call when you are ready to set things up."

As I watched her leave I knew that I would be calling her before the week was over. I needed to release some tension and if the woman I was set up with was a quarter as beautiful as Danni then I would be in ecstasy before school started Monday.

Saturday night I was picked up in front of a Wal-Mart in a minivan. The driver, Stacy, was pretty enough but she wasn't Danni. As we pulled in front of the attractive brownstone nervousness filled my stomach and desire filled my dick.

I knocked on the bright red door once, twice, then four times before a man answered. I showed him my membership ID and waited to be escorted to my private room. After receiving a call on his cell, the guard led me to a room and knocked on the door before quickly retreating, never saying a word the entire time.

The door slowly opened and I hesitantly entered. Once my eyes had adjusted to the darkness, I realized that I had stepped into my deepest BDSM fantasy.

Racks, fuck machines, tape, rope, whips, chains, handcuffs and anything else I could have ever imagined was arranged in front of me. I took all of this in before my mind and body zeroed in on a lone figure in the corner of the room. I inherently knew that if I wanted her to come to me I'd have to demand it.

"Come here," I said. She didn't move. "COME HERE," I yelled forcefully and finally the woman moved closer to me. The light hit her face and recognition set in. "Danni?"

"Yes Sir," she whispered, her head bowed.

I was speechless. There before me was the woman who had haunted my dreams for the last few days. Her chocolate skin gleamed in the white crotchless thong and half bra, her nipples exposed for my pleasure.

I reached out and rolled one between my fingers, she gasped. Then I pinched one between my fingernails with enough pressure to cause pain but not break her delicate skin, she moaned deeply. Roughly, I pushed her away from me and undressed, my eyes never leaving her. Grabbing her by her short hair, I pulled her to the middle of the room.

Two sets of cuffs were suspended by chains from the ceiling. I placed each of Danni's hands in the restraints and placed a ball gag in her mouth, preventing speech.

"Since you are unable to speak, if at any point you want to stop you will lift your right leg. You can scream, you can even cry and I will not stop but the moment you lift that right leg in the air I will free you and you can leave. Shall we begin?"

I walked to the corner of the space and brought over a rolling table filled with supplies. Whips, floggers, pumps, pinchers, vibrators, dildos, lubes and creams filled the space. A sense of total domination engulfed me. Not because I could do whatever I wanted to Danni but that she trusted me enough to make the decisions regarding pain and pleasure. Regardless of the amount of money a person paid, to give up that control and knowing at any time they could harm you yet you willingly submit was a scary thing to do.

Snapping out of my reverie, I grabbed the nipple pumps and connected them to her breasts. Danni's moans increased as I repeatedly depressed the pump, increasing the suction. I watched in silent astonishment as her nipples plumped then elongated inside the tube. Her high pitched scream let me know that pain had replaced pleasure and I released her. Before she could catch her breath I applied two nipple clamps that were connected by a thin chain onto the swollen tips. Again, her screams assaulted my ears.

"Did I ask you to utter a sound?" Promptly, she quieted down. "Good girl."
I stood soundlessly beside Danni as she got accustomed to the clamps. Soon, she was writhing wildly against the air and I knew that the pleasure had returned. The pressure on her nipples resonated in her core, heightening her arousal. I blindfolded her before reaching for a flogger and circled her.

I knew she could feel my heat and hear my heavy breathing. I let the strips of leather trail up and down her spine and over her thick thighs. I waited until she was completely relaxed before I slapped her voluptuous ass.

Blow after blow landed on her quivering flesh while moans flowed in a continuous stream from her parted lips. The red welts on her mocha ass turned me on more than words could express. Sweat poured from both of our bodies and she raised her ass and spread her legs in blatant invitation.

For the first time that night I actually listened to Danni's request. I ripped of her panties before turning my attention back to the cart and picking up my next item of pleasure. Gathering the moisture from her honeyed lips, I coated the bulb shaped plastic and slowly inserted in her ass. Watching her writhe and moan, set off fireworks in my body. There was nothing more beautiful than a woman who can submit herself to a man and enjoy it.

Making sure I was protected, I slipped inside her from behind. I held on to the chains and pumped vigorously. Low growls rippled from my parted lips as caramel skin pounded into chocolate. This was ecstasy, this was craziness, this was a fantasy come true.

Blood pounded in my ears and my vision became cloudy as I felt the rhythmic pulsing of Danni's orgasm. Even in the bedroom, my wife would be the dominant one, I could never be on top. To know that my movements could bring a woman to climax sent my confidence level into space.

Quickly, I pulled out of her and discarded the condoms before releasing her from the restraints. Automatically, she knew what I wanted. I watched in rapture as her pouty lips surrounded my throbbing dick. She held my gaze while sliding me in and out of her oral cavity. Soft whimpers left her lips as I continuously touched the back of her throat. I tried in vain to hold the inevitable.

The sooner I reached climax the sooner I'd have to leave and I didn't want this fantasy to end. I didn't want the cold, unyielding reality to slap me in the face once I stepped outside the Red Door.

I tried to hold it in but when her mouth widened and captured my dick and both balls I was done for. My body shuddered uncontrollably as I watched her swallow every drop. Slowly, she released me while I held on to the chains for support, my knees still quaking.

"Thank you," I whispered hoarsely.

"You're welcome," she whispered back. "I don't usually get involved with customers." Somehow I knew that about her. I knew that this was as much a fantasy for her as it was for me. "I appreciate the fact you would do this for me."

An amicable silence engulfed us as I dressed. Danni slipped on her robe and walked me to the door, her steps visibly labored. As we reached the exit I forcefully pulled her hair and kissed her hard before pushing her away from me.

"See you in couple of months, Danni."

"Wait," she practically begged. Not bothering to turn around, I waited for her to finish. "I have a proposition for you."

Turning around, I waited for her to continue. She was looking down at the ground, nervously biting her bottom lip. "Well?"

"Well...I, um...I know you only have a certain amount of times you can come here a year but I was wondering if you could come every week. I would waive the fee."

"And?" I asked. When it came to women like Danni there was always something else.

"And, if you like it maybe we can arrange for you to meet some of my women clientele."

Ahh, and there it was. In exchange for dominating her, I had to service her clients. I leaned back against the door and mulled it over. I knew that one night every few months with Danni would never be enough. However, selling myself to the highest bidder just to be with her wasn't the best option.

"I'll do it, on two conditions. You're mine. You don't let anyone touch, kiss or be inside of you. I have exclusive rights to your body. Also, I get to decide which of these ladies I will be involved with."

"Deal," she quickly agreed.

I left the dark room and headed to the front door where Stacy was waiting for me. As we drove through the suburban streets, a bittersweet feeling overcame me. I knew that my relationship would be over in a matter of months, along with my career. There was no way I could keep up this façade of meekness; when I was in complete control at Red Door. Something would have to give. And I didn't mind losing my bitch fiancé and bullshit career to be with Danni.

Late at night, if you drive forty-five minutes from the city of Chicago and down Heroin Highway, you'll find a small town where big dreams can come true. Dreams so taboo, so forbidden, people would pay an insane amount of money to keep them buried.

Welcome to Red Door, where our motto is "We'll treat you right...for a price." We will do our best to bring your fantasy so fruition as long as you keep your mouth shut, respect the employees, and, most importantly, never cross Danni.

Author's Note

Red Door, the novel, coming in Spring 2013.

Can't Get Enough

A heated sensation trickled down my spine, goose bumps formed on my arms and butterflies swarmed my stomach as I reached for a book off the library's top shelf. Turning around, I came face-to-face with the most beautiful man I had ever seen in my life. Café au lait skin over hard muscles on a six foot frame, chocolate eyes framed by wire rimmed glasses and deep dimples; one either side of a bright smile had my body going into overdrive.

Our eyes connected and he moved closer. I hoped that he was coming to talk to me but I wasn't hopeful. A man like that would never be seen with a woman like me. I wasn't tall, willowy and model like. I was average height with full breasts and hips. My smooth dark chocolate skin and naturally curly hair garnered me plenty of admiration but I knew that a man like him would go for the light-bright type of women with straight hair down to their asses.

I returned my attention back to the books when I felt a sensual heat envelope me. "Excuse me; I hope I didn't scare you off."

My heart raced in my chest as I slowly rotated my head to the left. Clearing my throat, I lowered my arms. "No, you didn't scare me," I whispered.

Extending his hand, he blessed me with that radiant smile. "Hi, I'm Victor Wallace but everyone calls me Red."

"Nakia Thomas, but everyone calls me Mocha," I said, shaking his large hand. A tingling sensation shot up my arm and I quickly released his hand. From the narrowing of his eyes I knew he felt it too.

"It's nice meeting you, Nakia. I saw you and wanted to introduce myself."

"Nice meeting you as well, Victor."

I attempted to turn around but his hand caught my wrist, preventing any further movement. "Please call me Red. I was wondering if you'd like to get a cup of coffee."

Indecision had me in its grip. I bit my lip nervously while trying to come up with a reason to say no but came up short. His hands on my body and my senses overwhelmed by his woodsy scent prevented me from forming a complete thought.

"Please don't say no."

The sincerity in his voice and on his face convinced me, not that I needed much convincing. "Sure."

Picking up the stack of books next to me, he took my hand in his free one and led me to the checkout station. My hand still in his, we walked into the warm March air, the eyes of envious women following us.

Weeks passed and turned into months. Coffee turned into dinner and dinner into dating. A relationship developed and love followed soon after. We went from Victor and Nakia to Red and Mocha. We were together so often that you could not say one's nickname without saying the other's. It was as if were one entity instead of two separate human beings.

Lifting my head to the July sun, I buried my bare feet in the Georgia soil. I raised my hands to the sky and stretched, while letting my toes sink deeper into the Georgia clay. My floral maxi dress fluttered in the slight breeze that carried the scent of lilacs and caressed my damp skin. Rain was in the air.

Without turning around I knew that Red was coming into my backyard. I could feel him. That was the thing about Red and me, we were connected. The heat from his body permeated my personal space as his arms wrapped around my waist. Leaning into him, I caressed his intertwined fingers.

"You should come inside. It's about to rain," he whispered before planting kisses along the side of my neck.

Offering him more of my neck, I sighed contentedly. "I like the rain. It washes my stress away."

"Mine too, but I don't want you catching a cold."

Moaning, I ran my fingernails lightly up his arms. It had been a long week for the both of us. We both ran our own business. I was a florist and he was a publicist. Being a business owner at any age was challenging but even more so when you were still in your twenties. Clients tended not to take you as seriously.

Rain drops fell from the sky in warm droplets as we swayed to a rhythm only we could hear. Turning in his arms, I wrapped my arms around Red's neck and kissed him deeply. His large hands ran up and down the length of my spine, heating my body.

Fisting his reddish brown hair, I sighed in pleasure as his hands made contact with my fevered skin. Lips still connected, I backed him up to an outdoor lounge chair and laid my body on top of his.

Labored breathing, whispers of fabric being shed from overheated bodies and distant thunder were the only sounds in our sensual paradise.

Overgrown pecan and peach trees created an exotic canopy above us, sheltering us from the outside world.

Rolling over, I wrapped my legs around Red's narrow waist and he cupped my ample ass. The rough texture of his tongue caressed my achy nipples. The sensation sent my mind into overdrive and created a sticky sweetness between my thighs. I watched in hazy pleasure as Red kissed and licked his way lower, stopping momentarily at my navel and pelvic bone.

Separating my thick thighs, he swore softly at the sight of my arousal. He stood and plucked a ripe peach from above us and bit into the juicy fruit, the juice trailing down his chiseled chin. Lowering himself between my thighs, he placed each leg on his shoulder and pulled my bottom until he was eye level with my dripping pussy.

Red took another bite of the fruit and placed the chunk inside me while manipulating my swollen clit with his free hand. Piece after piece of the fruit disappeared inside me, while my severely aroused body was taken on a sensual journey only Red could navigate.

An intense orgasm tore screams from my lips, mingling with the thunder. Waves of peach flavored cream left my quaking core as the rain temporarily soothed my inflamed body only for Red to stoke it again.

Lowering his face between my shaking thighs, Red sucked each piece of honey coated fruit from me. My head thrashed about the chair and my fingers pulled and teased my hard nipples. Slurps and gulps floated from the juncture of my thighs to my ears, scorching my brain.

"Peaches and cream, my favorite," he said, licking the fluids from his lips and chin.

Hurriedly, I pulled him down on top of me and kissed him, tasting myself. Not wanting to waste another second, I grabbed his rock hard dick and placed him inside my tight body. Contented sighs left both sets of my lips. Red buried his face in the crook of my neck.

I matched him stroke for stroke. My nails dug into his back and bit his shoulder to keep from wailing. The skies opened up and poured on us, but it was nothing compared to the wetness Red produced from me. Sweat, rain and arousal soaked the both of us.

"Shit, Mo…Damn, this is so good."

I could only moan in response. I could not have formed a coherent sentence even if my life depended on it. That was what he did to me, turned me into a pile of whimpering sexual neediness. I needed this. I needed this connection to get through my day. No matter how much I had him, I needed more. I simply couldn't get enough of Red.

Flipping on to his back, he took me with him. "Ride me, Mocha. Take me to another world."

How could I deny such an eloquent request? Bracing my hands on his sculpted shoulders, I rocked back and forth. Reds hands moved from my slim waist to my bouncing breasts and tweaked my hard nipples. Groans bubbled from my soul into the universe.

Eyes closed, head thrown back I bounced frantically on his dick. My greedy pussy gripped and clenched him until grunts and growls escaped his full lips. Climax was on the horizon. Faster and faster I moved my hips while the warm rain continued to assault our bodies. The scent of rain, damp soil, lilacs, peaches and sex encased us.

"Cumming!" I screamed. My entire body shook as if I had been electrocuted.

Red held me tight as he continued to pound my body until I squirted honey all over him, setting off his own orgasm. Lava erupted from him and filled me to capacity. Of their own volition his hips continued to pump into me while my core continued to milk him, both trying to wring the last remaining vestiges of pleasure from each other.

Gathering me tightly, Red carried me into my ranch style house and into the bedroom, our bodies still connected. Lying down in the bed, he pulled the down comforter over our wet bodies and ran his hands through my rain soaked curls. Rubbing my hands lightly up his arms, I allowed the heat from my man and the sound of the rain to lull me to a blissful sleep.

"Love looks good on you, Mo."

Glancing up from the arrangement I was working on, I smiled at my mother. "Thanks, Mom."

My mother, Jillian Thomas, had raised me by herself after my father died when I was nine years old. Fifteen years later, we were still very close. Nothing could tear us apart. That included Red. Though I loved him deeply, if my mother didn't like him then he would be out the door.

It was the last weekend in July and my mother's annual cookout. I invited Red and this would be the first time he would meet any member of my large family, including my mother. Anticipation and anxiety filled my stomach to the brim, threatening to make my breakfast resurface.

The doorbell rang, forcing me to regroup. The heels of my four inch cream Valentino platform sandals created a rhythm against the tiled floor that my hips swayed in time to, the skirt of my green and pink sundress fluttering around my knees. Opening the door to the two-story home I grew up in, I let in the loud and smiling relatives.

Food, liquor, and classic R&B set the mood for a good time. The summer sun beamed down on us and the blue sky was cloudless. I sat on the front porch, licking the sweet and sticky barbeque sauce from my fingertips, when the familiar tingling of awareness filled my body.

I looked up and my gaze collided with a heated chocolate one. Setting my plate on the wicker end table, I stood and waited. Dressed casually in green cargo shorts, a fitted white tee and a fresh pair of white Air Yeezys he looked amazingly handsome. As usual, Red ignored where we were and took me in his arms, giving me the kiss I had been craving since I left his bed that morning.

Hesitantly breaking off the heated kiss, I ran my fingers down his cheek. "Missed you."

"Missed you more. I'm nervous to meet your family."

I kissed him on his cheek before grabbing his hand. "Don't be. They'll love you."

I led him into the house and began introductions. Everyone took to him immediately. Wading through the crowded house, I looked for my mom. I wanted her and Red to finally meet. Though I was old enough and independent enough to make my own decisions I still wanted her approval. Finally, I found her sitting on a sofa on the back porch with her two sisters and my grandmother, all the matriarchs in one place.

"Excuse me, mom, grandma and aunties. I would like to introduce to you to my boyfriend, Victor." Turning to Red, I smiled. "Red, I would like you to meet my grandmother, Rose Lemont, my mother, Jillian Thomas, and my aunts, Sadie Morgan and Tiffany Brown."

"Nice to meet all of you," he said while shaking their hands.

Sitting down in the wicker chairs in front of them, I waited for the interrogation to begin. Aunt Tiffany did not disappoint.

"So, Victor, what do you do?"

"I own my own business, I am a publicist."

"Mmhm, where do live?"

"I actually, live down the street from here. Augusta isn't that big," he chuckled, no one else joined in.

"Apartment or house?"

Clearing his throat, he wiped his sweaty palms on his shorts. "I own a house."

My grandmother placed a hand on Aunt Tiffany's knee, signaling that her time to speak was up. "What are your intentions with my granddaughter?"

"My intentions are all honorable I assure you."

"Elaborate," my mother hissed.

"Mama!" I exclaimed. I couldn't believe she was being so nasty.

"No baby, it's okay. I love Nakia. I think that we are on the path to something greater, more permanent."

"You think or you know?" My mother's hard eyes assessed Red. My mother was usually mild mannered and easy going. I had never seen her dislike someone so quickly. My heart plummeted into my stomach.

Leaning forward in his seat, Red met my mother's stare head on. "I know that I want to make it more permanent." My pulse began to race. "We've only begin together for a short while but once we've been together for a while longer I will ask her to marry me."

Standing abruptly, my mother smoothed her tank top over her flat stomach. "Excuse me," she said quickly before walking quickly into the house.

"Red, I'm sorry, give me a minute." Taking off after my mother, I found her in the empty kitchen. Her hands were braced on the edge of the sink, her head bowed. "Mama, what was that?"

"Not now, Mocha."

"Yes, now!! Why were you so rude to him?"

She turned around quickly with a wild look in her eyes. "Because I know his type. He's just going to leave you. That's what men like him do, why can't you see that?"

"What do you mean men like him?" I was truly confused.

"Pretty men, Mocha. Pretty men like him don't come after women like us without an ulterior motive. With his fair skin, funny colored hair and chiseled features he will find some light-bright bitch to be with soon enough."

"So…because I'm darker he shouldn't like me, want to be with me? You always told me that color didn't matter, that it made us all unique. Now you're telling me that I'm not good enough for Red? You are some piece of work."

Grabbing my hands roughly, she got all in my personal space. "Mocha this is the south, color will always matter here. Light skinned men marry light skinned women. He'll just use you for a while then find some light bright, wavy haired floozy to be with and you'll be sitting right here with me crying your eyes out."

"Red won't do that to me," I said but the seeds of doubt had already been planted in my head.

"Yeah, he will and when he does don't say that I didn't warn you."

There is a moment in every relationship when the outside world begins to creep in and cast a shadow over the sunny lover's paradise you and your boo created. If meeting my mother was the shadow; then meeting Red's family was a motherfucking solar eclipse.

I was still reeling from the conversation with my mother two months prior when Red informed me that we were invited to his mother's home for a family get together. I was extremely nervous.

Though our town of Augusta, GA wasn't as big as Atlanta it was still easy to get lost in the crowd. I had never met any of Red's family. We grew up on different sides of the city, went to different schools and had different sets of friends. If we hadn't met in the library we probably would have never known that the other existed. That thought caused my heart to plummet to my stomach and seize with pain.

The night of the party I made sure to dress with care. The temperature had finally taken a dip down to a cool seventy degrees compared to the high nineties we experienced during the summer.

A knee length, cap shoulder purple lace dress skimmed my curves while five inch silver pumps and large silver hoop earrings completed the look. My wild curls were secured with a headband, allowing a clear view of my face that held subtle makeup.

I turned towards the mirror and spritzed on my favorite perfume, filling the air with the scent of orange blossoms and amber.

Looking in the mirror, I caught the appreciative gleam in Red's eyes. A low whistle rushed from his parted lips. "Baby, you look good as hell." He glanced at his watch. "We have thirty minutes before we have to leave. Why don't we relax for a while?"

Rolling my eyes, I expertly applied clear gloss to my pouty lips. "I don't think so. It took me forever to tame this hair. I don't want to have to do it again because you want to relax." I turned towards him and smiled. "You look good too."

And he did. Dark washed jeans held up by a chocolate leather belt sat on his narrow hips. A pale blue sweater over a starched white dress shirt showed off his wide shoulders. Walking over to me in his chocolate loafers, he nuzzled my neck.

"No, Red, we can't," I breathed as I shamelessly rubbed my body against him.

He suckled my earlobe, inhaling my perfume deeply. "Your mouth says no but your body says yes."

I grabbed his head, intending to push him away but I only brought him closer. My legs wrapped around his waist and indulged in his touches a while longer before extracting myself from his grasps. Our eyes met in the mirror, his full of smoldering heat and mine full of barely constrained submission. I knew that if we didn't leave now we wouldn't leave at all.

Bypassing Red, I grabbed my lightweight ankle length coat and my small black sequined clutch from the bed and waited in the car. As we drove through the semi-busy streets of Augusta I felt a sense of inner peace.

Just being around Red could calm my erratic nerves. Though I had not had a lot of men in my life I knew it was rare to find one who understood you on an elemental level, whose mere presence could bring out the best in you.

For that, I would ignore my mother's taunting warning. Nothing and no one could destroy the harmony we had created in a few short months.

Three hours later I was singing a different tune. Red's mother had systematically extinguished the sensual flames Red and I had created earlier in the evening. I had to give it to Tameka Wallace, she was a slick one.

She wasn't like my mother who would cause a scene at the drop of a hat to ruin something she didn't like. No, she liked to get into her victim's, yes, I said victim, heads and let them demolish it themselves. Her hands never got dirty.

Tameka Wallace's sideways glances, her refusing to touch me and her condescending laughter had done what no one had been able to accomplish since I was a child, make me feel insecure.

For example, when I told her that I owned a successful flower shop she simply looked at me and said, "So, you like to be outside and play in dirt all day."

To anyone else it would have seemed like a comment born from the lack of knowledge about the floral industry. I knew better. It was a house slave/field slave reference.

See, in the minds of some black people, there was still this invisible divide between dark and light skin blacks that should not be crossed. Red's

those narrow minded people. If
with myself I would say that my
the same way.

Entering the bedroom, I mindlessly stripped
m my pretty dress and killer heels while Red
talked endlessly about his family and childhood
memories. He was so caught up walking down
memory lane that he didn't notice my distress.

Turning down the comforters, I laid my
emotionally exhausted body against the cool silk
sheets. Red got into bed and spooned me from
behind, his hand automatically palming my breasts.
His soft snores pulled me into a sleep that I hoped
would calm my fears.

I woke up the next morning to find my body
sprawled across the length of his. Our legs
intertwined, my face buried in his neck and my
arms wrapped tight around him, clinging to him as
if I was afraid I'd wake up and our relationship
would be nothing but a dream.

The bell over my shop door rang, signaling the arrival of a customer. Wiping my hands on my smock, I stopped working on the bridal bouquet I had been slaving over for the last two hours and made my way to the front.

As soon as I entered the room, all the air rushed from my lungs, my temperature spiked and my body felt clammy. Red leaned leisurely against the sales counter looking better than any man had a right to.

His hair was closely cropped to his scalp and his goatee, that he recently grew, was freshly lined. A charcoal grey Ralph Lauren suit did nothing to distract from his rugged sexiness, it just enhanced it. In short, Red looked like sex personified.

Unconsciously, I licked my lips and watched his eyes zero in on my tongue's movements. Turning, he locked the door and put up the "Out to Lunch" sign before turning his attention back to me.

Grabbing my hand, he led me to the back room and closed the door. I leaned against the workspace and we stared at each other for a few heated moments before he came to me. No words were needed but he said them anyways, "I need you. I couldn't wait until you got home."

⌐ his voice almost brought me to
⌐ad just made love that morning. To
⌐ couldn't get enough of me made me
⌐wered and erased any insecurity I felt
⌐ing our relationship.

I wrapped my arms around his muscular
frame, enjoying the heat and the closeness. Red
untied the strings to my smock and it landed to floor
with a whisper. Running my hands down his torso,
I unbuttoned his black shirt and loosened the black
and grey tie. Hints of light brown skin appeared
before my eyes, making my tongue feel heavy with
the need to taste and my hands itchy with the need
to feel.

Red's hands were as busy as my own. The
polo shirt with my company's logo was on the floor
next to the smock. My jeans and shoes were in a
pile near our feet, leaving me clad only in a nude
and black lace bra and panty set. Removing my
hands from his belt buckle, Red stepped back and
looked at me. I was spread out on the workspace,
my knees bent and my feet perched on the edge, for
his viewing pleasure. I had no shame where he was
concerned.

Stepping closer to me, he ripped my panties
from my body and brought them to his nose before
inhaling deeply. His eyes fluttered and closed while

his head fell back on his neck. The arousal in his pants strained against the zipper and his breathing escalated. I had never seen anything so unbearably provocative in my life.

Unable to take another second, I lightly teased my own damn nipples until they were rock hard. At my soft moan Red's eyes snapped open. He stared at me, turning me on even more. I loved having an audience but I loved having him inside me more.

Spreading my legs wider, I opened my moist folds and revealed the bubblegum pink center. "Red, please. I need you."

As soon as the words left my mouth his entire body reacted. Red's eyes narrowed, nostrils flared, and jaw ticked. His already snug pants seemed ready to burst as he swelled further. His fingers fumbled as he undid his belt and zipper, the jingle of the belt and rasp of the zipper my own personal symphony of sexual triumph.

Standing in front of my spread thighs, he let go of his hold on his pants and they fluttered to his feet. He placed one then two fingers inside me while he shimmied out of his boxers and sheathed himself. Screams of ecstasy tore from both sets of swollen lips as he entered me swiftly.

This was what a damn afternoon delight felt like! Hips pressed into each other, bodies connected so deeply you'd have to pry us apart. Red's hands cradled my head and lower back while my nails bit into his back. Silently I cursed the cotton fabric that prevented my fingers from dancing across his fevered skin.

"You with me, Mo?" he asked, biting my earlobe.

"All the way, Daddy, all the fucking way."

His deep chuckle had me swiveling my hips faster. "Damn, this pussy is good, girl." Leaning back, he looked in my eyes. The same emotions that I knew swirled in my chocolate orbs swam in his, vulnerability and love. "You're mine, Mo. This is mine."

"God, yes!" I screamed, climax gripping tightly.

Growls erupted from Red's chest as shrieks bubbled from mine. This was sex at its finest. This was animalistic, this was love, this was unabashed, unashamed, unadulterated orgasmic bliss.

Reluctantly, Red pulled his still throbbing dick from my quaking pussy, my honey dripping from him in sticky droplets. The scent of exotic flowers and sex wafted into my nostrils, I moaned deeply. Red looked at me as he straightened his clothing and the pulse in his throat jumped. Instinctively I knew that if we had more time he'd be back inside me before I had a chance to utter another sound. Unfortunately, since we both had work to do that was not possible.

In silence we both tried to make ourselves look as presentable as possible. Secret touches and lingering glances made the process longer than it should have been. Hand in hand we walked to the front and he kissed me. It was brief but I felt it to my toes. With promises of picking up where we left off tonight, I watched him leave and took the sign off the door.

Turning to finish working on the bridal bouquet, I walked to the back when the bell chimed again. I entered the sales space and came face to face with Tameka Wallace. Seeing her had officially blown my sexual high and put my defenses up.

Determined to behave in the dignified way my mother had taught me, I smiled. "How can I help you today, Mrs. Wallace?"

"You can help me by ending this foolish affair with my son."

So, we're getting straight to the point, I thought to myself. "No." Ignoring her gasp and the daggers her eyes threw at me, I continued, "What else can I help you with? How about some nice roses or orchids?"

"I don't want your flowers," she hissed. The real Tameka Wallace was coming out to play. "I want you to leave my son alone. You've had your fun. He's satisfied his curiosity. Now, he needs to find a suitable wife and he can't do that if you keep sniffing around him."

Keeping the saccharine smile on my face, I looked her right in her evil eyes. "I'm not sniffing around your son. He is a grown man and more than capable of breaking up with a woman if he feels the need. Obviously he loves me, otherwise he would have been gone. We're not having an affair and he's not satisfying a curiosity, we are in a relationship."

"Look here, you black bitch. I tried to be nice about this but since you can't seem to get it let me be clear. You are not going to be with my son. I'll be damned if I have a bunch of pickaninny grandchildren running around town ruining my family name."

If I wasn't sure I'd go to jail I would have slapped that bitch. "Mrs. Wallace," I spat, "I think it's time for you to go."

Tightening her hand around the strap of her Louis Vuitton purse, she glared at me. "Stay away from my son, tar baby."

"Or what?" I asked with my hands on my hips and my voice full of attitude.

"Or there will be hell to pay."

"Are you threatening me?"

"No, I'm making you a promise."

With that, the evil racist bitch slammed my door and disappeared in the cool fall air.

A light dusting of snow covered the ground on Christmas day. It had been a month since I had seen Mrs. Wallace and I was glad. I didn't tell Red about the incident in the flower shop because I didn't know how he would react or if he would even believe. Men had a tendency to think their mother's shit didn't stink.

Stretching leisurely, I hopped out of my bed and made my way to the kitchen. Red was in the shower, singing off key as usual, and I prepared his favorite breakfast of bacon, eggs, grits and biscuits. The coffee had just finished brewing when he walked his fine ass in the kitchen in just a robe.

If we didn't have to get to church, I would have rode him like one of Santa's reindeer. Red had me good and whipped and he knew it but I wasn't complaining. I had his ass wrapped around my little finger.

After enjoying a hearty breakfast I was about to make my way to the shower when he grabbed my wrist. "I want you to open your gift now."

"I thought we were going to do this tonight with my family?"

"Yeah," he said, pulling me to the couch. "But I changed my mind."

Rolling my eyes, I sat on the fiery orange sofa and waited for him to give me the gift. He placed a rectangle box in my lap. I carefully peeled back the silver and gold wrapping paper and revealed a rectangle black box. Arching a brow, I glanced at him but he just smiled. Opening the box, I gasped.

In the box, laid across satin were twenty diamond and precious stone engagement rings, each one different than the others. Tears sparkled in my eyes and Red knelt in front of me.

"Pick one," he whispered.

"Are you sure?" Uncertainty lined my voice. We had only been together nine months.

"I've never been surer of anything in my life." Taking my left hand in his, he stared into my watery eyes. "I love you. I love everything about you. I love the way you walk, the way you talk, the way your eyes light up when you're excited, the way you always smell like flowers, the way you play with your hair when you're nervous, the way you're doing now."

I quickly pulled my hand down to my lap.

"I love the way you believe in me and support me. I love the way you find the good in people. I love how you don't let anything stop you from achieving your goals. I love the way I feel when I hold you. I love the way your skin gleams in the sunlight. I love how your hair caresses my skin. I love the way you taste. Nakia, I even love your mother, though she hates me."

I chuckled softly, tears cascading down my cheeks.

"I love everything about you, Nakia. Will you please make an honest man of me?" Throwing my arms around his neck, I screamed yes. "Pick one," he said, nodding towards the rings.

Taking a deep breath, I stared at the rows of rings in front of me. Biting my lower lip, I selected a sapphire and white diamond ring set in platinum. With shaky hands Red placed it on the third finger on my left hand and kissed me deeply.

For the rest of the day I floated on cloud nine. Congratulations poured in from both of our families, some more sincere than others. Lying in Red's arms later that night, I couldn't help but recall the reaction of Mrs. Wallace when she heard the news. She had cried hysterically. Red thought it was because she was so elated but I knew the truth.

When Red left to get her a glass of water and a Kleenex; she wasted no time telling me not to get too comfortable and that I would be on my way out the door sooner rather than later. All I did was hold up my left hand and admire my ring which set off another round of tears.

I wouldn't delude myself into thinking that the issue of my skin color was over. From what I had gathered around town Tameka Wallace wasn't nothing to fuck with. I may had won the battle but we were just getting started with the war. But until then, I would continue to get my fill of Red.

Straddling his thighs, I placed his hardening member inside me and rode him hard. Slowly opening his eyes, a yawn fell from his lips before a deep moan. "Damn, Mo, you're horny again?"

"I...uhh...I can't get enough."

Author's Note

Racial lines within the black community are more prevalent than most would think. Light skin versus dark skin is an issue that dates back to slavery and is still relevant today. Obviously, this story is just the beginning of the journey between Red and Mocha.

Red and Mocha Blues Summer 2013.

PHOENIX'S FINAL THOUGHTS

Love and sex are probably the two most addictive drugs on the planet. Once you get that first taste it is hard to stop. Each of these stories depicted the troubles that come when you become Whipped. Though problems can arise when you become addicted to another person I believe that the addiction is the mystique behind any relationship.

I'm not saying that being Whipped is either good or bad. What I am saying is that as long as you are not in denial then maybe just maybe your high will last a long time.

PHOENIX WILLIAMS

Turn the page for a sneak peak at the story Robin that will appear in the book Screwed, released December 2012.

<u>ROBIN</u>

"So, Mary's daughter, Valerie, just got married."

Oh God, here it comes, I thought to myself.

"Mary couldn't stop talking about the wedding. I wish I could plan a wedding. When are you going to finally settle down, Robin?"

There it is. My mother, Tianna "T" Bird, was constantly on my case about getting married. It was worse than ever since my younger sisters were now in relationships. My sister, Raven, had been married to her husband, Dean, for ten years. My younger sister, Sparrow, was now in a legitimate relationship with her boyfriend, Isaiah, and it looked promising. I was the only one of my sisters alone.

"Mama, I don't know when I'm going to get married. I guess when the right man comes along I'll know."

Taking a sip of her tea, my mother leaned back into the wicker chair while the August sun shined on her jet black hair. "It's not like you're unattractive. You have a nice shape, good hair and a gorgeous face. You are part owner of one of the most successful interior design companies in the state. I don't understand how you don't even have a boyfriend and your sisters do."

Drowning out my mother's tirade, I thought about my sisters. Sparrow was my youngest sister and a total knockout. She was 5'10" and had a caramel complexion, big breasts, fat ass, brownish gold hair, full lips and brown eyes. At 27, she had finally found a man that she loved but it hadn't always been that way. Instead of naming her Sparrow, my parents should have named the bitch Swallow. She had more men between both sets of lips than I cared to count.

My sister Raven, my parents should have named her ass Cuckoo because only a dumbass would get themselves in the mess that she had. Raven was 29 and your typical supermodel type, tall and willowy with small breasts and small hips. She also lacked common sense. As much as she tried to deny it, we all knew her husband Dean, was a drug dealer.

Despite one being a whore and the other a dumbass both of my sisters had managed to do what I could not, capture the love a man. Yeah, men wanted to sleep with me but none wanted to be with me. It was hard knowing that I lacked something especially when everyone around me had it. Even my mother was in a relationship, though it wasn't a happy one.

Tianna "T" Bird had been married to my father, Jay Bird, for over thirty years. She had stood by his side while he went to school, built his practice and continuously cheated on her. My mother was one of those traditional women who didn't believe in divorcing a man for being a man. As she would say, "When a woman loves…" I truly hoped to love someone as much as my mother loved my father though I wouldn't condone the infidelity.

Snapping out of my reverie, I brushed my sandy brown hair out of my eyes. "Mom, I know you want to plan my wedding and I would love for you to do it. However, until I find a man to marry there is nothing I can do."

"Don't worry, baby," she said with a smile. "I'll help you find someone."

Sighing with resignation, I knew that my mom was going to set me up with yet another one of her friend's sons, grandsons or employees. As much as I loathed being set up on a blind date I would do it anyway. My mother wanted grandchildren and since Dean and Raven didn't want kids and Sparrow was too busy, I would have to give them to her. As usual, I would try not to disappoint.

Two weeks later, I was waiting in a dimly lit restaurant in Chicago for my mom's friend's son, Matthew, to show up. This was the third blind date she had set me up on and hopefully the last. The first two did not go well at all.

The first guy, Troy, was overly arrogant and wanted to get me into his bed before the entrees had hit the table. His hands tried to grope my thick thighs for the fifth time before I finally had enough and left, but not before throwing my wine in his lap to cool him off.

The second guy, Lovell, had too much drama going on. Things had started off fine. We were getting along and the conversation was flowing but as we got ready to order desert his ex showed up. That wouldn't have been so bad if his ex wasn't a 6'2" ex-con named Tyrell.

It wasn't until that moment that I realized that Lovell was gay. I sat in shock watching Tyrell and Lovell argue. The finger snapping, neck rolling and teeth sucking were too much for me to handle. So, I left but not before Tyrell threw red wine on my favorite white pantsuit.

Checking my watch, I realized Matthew was fifteen minutes late. That was definitely not a good sign. I didn't want my future husband to be late without even a courtesy call or text. I mentally reviewed my appearance to make sure that I made a good first impression. I wore a smart black pantsuit that gave a tempting yet classy peek of my abundant cleavage and slightly hugged my hips and ample ass. Sensible shoes added two inches to my 5'6" frame. Light make up accentuated my high cheekbones and wide brown eyes.

"You must be Robin."

My head snapped up at the sound of the deep voice above me. I glanced up and was immediately disappointed. "Matthew?"

"In the flesh beautiful," he said. "I'm sorry I'm late. Just give me one second to use the restroom. I'll be right back."

As he walked away I knew that this would not go anywhere. Matthew was shorter than me without my heels. His voice was a cross between baritone and nasal. His butter toned skin was blotchy and scarred from acne. His goatee was patchy and he was balding. If I had to have guessed I would have thought he was in his forties. The icing on the cake was his smile. His teeth were the exact shade of his skin. I had to make an exit before I got stuck sitting here eating dinner with this man.

Coming back to the table, Matthew sat back in his seat and smiled that yellow smile at me. "So, your mom told me a lot about you."

"All good I hope," I said while trying to formulate a plan to leave without hurting his feelings.

"Most definitely. She told me that you were 32 and that you need to settle down. I'm 35 and I'm ready to settle down too. I figure we can help each other out."

Oh, my God, I thought to myself. "I'm sorry, I'm not following."

"Basically, you need a husband and I need a wife. I'm choosing you. Now, you don't have to worry about being alone and childless. What would you like to eat?" he asked, picking up the menu as if everything was settled between us and I could go buy a wedding gown.

Shock and anger were the only emotions I felt. Leaning close to him, I hissed, "Let's get something straight. Number one, I am not desperate for a man..."

"That's not what I heard," he interrupted.

"Number two, even if I was desperate I would not choose you."

Quickly, I gathered my things and stood to leave. "Robin, there's no reason to be indignant. Beggars can't be choosers. You're 32 and single with no prospects. I'm sure I'm not your dream man but I'm the only man willing to give you what you want, a family. Do me a favor tonight, okay? While you're in bed tonight, alone as usual, listen hard. I'm sure you'll be able to hear the ticking of your biological clock."

Storming out of the restaurant, I practically ran to my car. That man had a lot of nerve acting like he was my last resort. Yeah, I hadn't been in a relationship in four years and hadn't had sex in three but it wasn't as if I couldn't keep a man.

Sure, my standards were a little high and the last few dates I had been on ended in disaster but that didn't mean I would end up alone. It was just taking me a little longer to find my soul mate. As long as I held out the hope that my Mr. Right was out there then I would be fine.

I pulled up to my three story house in Naperville and went straight into my master bathroom. The sound of water hitting travertine and the air conditioner were the only sounds in the entire house. Loneliness cloaked me as I stripped from my clothing and the hot water from the shower to spray over me.

Matthew's comments continued to play in my head like a broken record and tears filled my eyes. As much as I pretended to be strong and accepting of my solitude, deep down I was filled to the rafters with isolation. It hurt so bad that at times I couldn't even breathe.

I exited the shower and slipped into my favorite flannel pajamas before entering my bedroom. My bedroom was definitely my place of solace. White carpeting and golden oak furniture gave the room a serene feel. The queen sized canopy bed was covered with a white bedspread and fluffy pillows while gold and white cloths draped from the canopy top. I slipped in between the covers and closed my eyes, the ticking of my biological clock and the cloak of loneliness lulling me to sleep.

Other titles by Phoenix Williams:

Running available on www.amazon.com

Screwed: 12/2012

Stripped: 01/2013

The LadyBird Chronicles: 03/2013

Red Door: Spring 2013

Red and Mocha Blues: Summer 2013

For more information about Phoenix Williams and her books please visit the sites below.

Facebook: www.facebook.com/phoenixwilliamsbooks

Twitter: www.twitter.com/phoenix_william

Email: phoenixwilliamsbooks@gmail.com

Blog: phoenixwilliams.blogspot.com

WHIPPED

PHOENIX WILLIAMS

Made in the USA
Charleston, SC
20 April 2013